Closing her eyes, she pressed a hand to her belly and breathed deeply, in and out.

Having inherited her mother's petite figure and danced for exercise most days of her life, her stomach had always been flat. Early though the pregnancy was, there was a noticeable swelling, just as her breasts had swollen. As dream-like as everything had felt these last few days, one thing had made itself felt with concrete certainty: she was pregnant. Her body was doing what it needed to do to bring her baby safely into this world. And Alessia would do what was needed too, and that meant marrying Gabriel.

She'd expected coming face-to-face with him to be hard, but she hadn't expected it to be that hard. She hadn't expected to feel so *much*.

Being a good, dutiful princess... That was Alessia's role in this world, her purpose, her reason for being.

Her night with Gabriel was a different matter entirely. That night, she had broken free from the bonds of duty and freed the real woman inside, and it was terrifying how strongly seeing Gabriel again relit that passionate fire inside her.

Scandalous Royal Weddings

Marriages to make front-page news!

Raised on the Mediterranean island kingdom of Ceres, Princes Amadeo and Marcelo and Princess Alessia want for nothing. But with their life of luxury comes an impeccable reputation to uphold. Any hint of a scandal could turn the eyes of the world on them...and force them down the royal aisle! Their lives may be lived in the spotlight, but only one person will have the power to truly see them...

When Prince Marcelo rescues Clara from a forced wedding, he simultaneously risks a diplomatic crisis and his heart.

Read on in
Crowning His Kidnapped Princess

Billionaire Gabriel may fix scandals for a living, but his night with Princess Alessia creates a scandal of their own when she discovers she's pregnant!

Read on in
Pregnant Innocent Behind the Veil

Both available now!

Prince Amadeo must face a stranger at the altar, when convenient royal wedding bells chime. Look out for his story, coming soon!

Don't miss this scandalous trilogy by Michelle Smart!

Michelle Smart

PREGNANT INNOCENT
BEHIND THE VEIL

HARLEQUIN

PRESENTS

Recycling programs
for this product may
not exist in your area.

ISBN-13: 978-1-335-73873-8

Pregnant Innocent Behind the Veil

Copyright © 2022 by Michelle Smart

For questions and comments about the quality of this book,
please contact us at CustomerService@Harlequin.com.

Harlequin Enterprises ULC
22 Adelaide St. West, 41st Floor
Toronto, Ontario M5H 4E3, Canada
www.Harlequin.com

Printed in U.S.A.

Michelle Smart's love affair with books started when she was a baby and would cuddle them in her cot. A voracious reader of all genres, she found her love of romance established when she stumbled across her first Harlequin book at the age of twelve. She's been reading them—and writing them—ever since. Michelle lives in Northamptonshire, England, with her husband and two young Smarties.

Books by Michelle Smart

Harlequin Presents

Stranded with Her Greek Husband
Claiming His Baby at the Altar

Billion-Dollar Mediterranean Brides

The Forbidden Innocent's Bodyguard
The Secret Behind the Greek's Return

The Delgado Inheritance

The Billionaire's Cinderella Contract
The Cost of Claiming His Heir

Christmas with a Billionaire

Unwrapped by Her Italian Boss

Scandalous Royal Weddings

Crowning His Kidnapped Princess

Visit the Author Profile page
at Harlequin.com for more titles.

This is for Mitchell. I hope life brings you an abundance of joy xxx

CHAPTER ONE

ALESSIA BERRUTI'S HAND shook as she pressed 'play' on her phone. The scene, one which had already been viewed by over two million people since its upload four hours earlier, was a wedding reception. Hundreds of finely dressed people were celebrating in a stateroom in the castle where the royal family of Ceres lived. The camera zoomed in on two women. The loud music and waves of surrounding conversation faded.

'Your brother looks smitten,' the blonde lady in the video footage said. Her voice, although pitched low, was clearly audible.

'He is.' The tiny, chestnut-haired woman who answered looked over her shoulder. The camera perfectly captured the face of Princess Alessia Berruti.

The blonde's voice dropped even lower. 'I wonder how Dominic's feeling right now, seeing his intended bride marry another man.'

'Who gives a...' A loud beep was dubbed over the princess's scathing retort. 'That man's an obese, sweaty, disgusting monster.'

'Don't hold back,' the blonde said with a laugh. 'Say what you really think.'

The princess laughed too and drank some more champagne before saying, 'Okay, what I *really* think is that King Dominic of Monte Cleure should be locked behind bars and never allowed within three kilometres of any woman ever again.'

The footage ended the moment Alessia's phone buzzed in her hand. It was her eldest brother, Amadeo.

'My quarters,' he said icily. 'Now.'

Four days later, Alessia covered her flaming face and wished for the chair she was sitting on to plunge her into a deep pit.

What had she done?

Trying her hardest not to cry again, she lifted her stare to Amadeo. His features were as taut and uncompromising as she had ever seen them. To his right, their mother, her expression as unyielding as her eldest son's. To their mother's right, their father, the only person in this whole room with a smidgeon of sympathy. She couldn't bring herself to look at the man sat on the other side of Amadeo, the final link in the human chain of disappointment and anger being aimed at her.

'I'm so sorry,' Alessia whispered for the third time. 'I had no idea I was being filmed.'

It was an excuse that cut no ice, not even with her.

One unguarded moment. That's all it had been. Unguarded or not, she should have known better. She *did* know better. Her whole life had been spent having her basic human desires and reactions restrained so that she was always in total control of herself.

'I'll marry Dominic,' she blurted into the silence. 'I'm the one who's got us into this mess, I'm the one who should be punished. Not you.'

That had been the king's first demand in the Berrutis' valiant efforts to make amends. Marriage to Princess Alessia. It would show the world, so he said, that she had been jesting and that the Berruti royal family respected him. That the world had already got wind that he'd once made overtures about marriage to the princess and been politely rebuffed mattered not a jot to him. King Dominic had thicker skin than a rhinoceros. He also had the vanity of a peacock and the cruelty of a medieval despot. So atrocious was his reputation that not a single eligible female member of any European royal family had agreed to a date, let alone marriage. Dominic's desperation for a blue-blooded bride had seen him trick a very distant relation of the current British monarch to his principality and then hold her hostage until she agreed to marry him. His victim escaped barely an hour before her forced nuptials when Alessia's other brother, Marcelo, rescued her to worldwide amazement and Dominic's fury, and married her for himself. It was at Marcelo and Clara's wedding reception that Alessia had opened her mouth and made the simmering relations between the two nations boil over.

'Don't think I've not been tempted,' Amadeo said grimly at the same moment their father stated, 'Out of the question.'

'But why should Amadeo have to give up his whole life for something that's my fault?' she implored.

'Because, sister,' Amadeo answered, 'tempting though it may be to insist you marry that man, I wouldn't marry someone I hate to him never mind my own sister.'

A tear leaked out and rolled down her cheek. She wiped it away. 'But this is *my* fault. Surely there's a way to make amends and bring peace to our countries without you having to do this?'

The man Alessia had been cursorily introduced to three days ago addressed her directly for the first time. 'This is the one resolution satisfactory to both parties.'

Gabriel Serres. The 'fixer' brought in by her parents and brother to fix the mess and bring peace to Ceres and Monte Cleure, and the most handsome man she'd ever laid eyes on. She'd taken one look at him and, for a few short moments, all her troubles had blown out of her mind.

For three days Gabriel had flown back and forth between their Mediterranean island and the European principality, negotiating between the two parties. Alessia, in disgrace for pouring fuel over the simmering tensions between the two nations, had, to her immense frustration, been cut off from the negotiations. Until now. When the deal was done.

Done deal or not, that didn't stop her arguing against it. 'How can Amadeo marrying a complete stranger be satisfactory?'

'The bride is the king's cousin. Their marriage will

unify the two nations, reopen diplomatic ties and prevent a costly trade war,' Gabriel reminded the princess with deliberate indifference.

His indifference was usually effortless. A man did
not reach the top of the diplomatic field by getting
emotionally involved in the disputes he was paid to
resolve, but he'd found himself having to work at
maintaining his usual detachment since Alessia had
entered the meeting room. Dressed in a pair of tight-
fitted, cropped black trousers topped with a loose,
white scooped top, her straight dark chestnut hair
hung loose around her shoulders. A puffiness to her
dark brown eyes suggested she'd been crying, and he
could see she was battling to maintain her composure. Like her mother, Queen Isabella, the princess
was tiny, more so in the flesh than in the constant
ream of photographs the press so loved to publish of
her. In the flesh, there was something about her that
brought to mind the spinning ballerina in his sister's
old musical jewellery box.

Since their introduction three days ago, he'd found
his mind wandering to her in ways that could not be
classed as professional. The few times he'd spotted
her in the distance had made him give double takes,
and he'd had to consciously stop himself from staring
at her. Yesterday, on a brief visit back to the castle,
he'd been getting out of his car when she'd appeared,
flanked by her bodyguards, clearly about to head off
somewhere. Their eyes had caught and held. Just for
a moment. But it had been moment enough for a fris-
son to race through his veins. It had been moment

enough for him to see the mirroring flash of awareness in her eyes.

He supposed any red-blooded man would find the princess attractive but it was a rare occasion Gabriel found himself noticing someone's desirability when working. Single-minded focus and a refusal to accept failure were traits that had helped make him one of the world's leading negotiators. There was not a top agency in the world that hadn't, at some point, called in his services. His services were simple—he acted as a bridge between warring peoples, be they businesses, government agencies or a division of the UN. His skills meant that disputes were resolved without either side losing face.

He charged a hefty fee for those services. A diplomatic Svengali who worked under the radar of the press, he also had a canny eye for start-ups with potential and, as such, his investments had made him rich beyond his wildest dreams. Gabriel Serres was the billionaire no one had heard of. Intensely private and disdaining of the celebrity-fixated world, this anonymity was exactly how he liked it. His affairs—though he disliked calling them affairs when they involved two consenting adults enjoying each other until the time came to move on—were conducted under the same intense bounds of privacy, and never with a client. To find himself attracted to his client's daughter, a woman who lived her life in the glare of a media circus, was disconcerting to say the least. Gabriel's childhood had been one huge media circus, and it was a state of being he'd actively avoided ever since.

'And what of his bride?' the object of his attraction bit out in the husky voice that evoked thoughts of dark, sultry rooms and sensual pleasure. 'Does she get a say in it? Or is she being married against her will and without her consent?'

Her anger and concern was genuine, he recognised. Princess Alessia Berruti, the darling of the European press, a woman who'd mastered the art of social media to display herself and her royal family in the best possible attention-grabbing light, was not as self-centred as he'd presumed.

'She has agreed to the marriage,' he assured her.

Gabriel's expression was indifferent, his smooth, accented voice—an accent Alessia couldn't place—dispassionate, but there was something about the laser of his brown stare and the timbre in his tone that sent a shiver racing up her spine. It was a shiver that managed to be warm and was far from unpleasant. For the beat of an instant, a connection passed between them, sending another warm shiver coiling through her. But then he snapped his eyes shut and when they next locked on hers, the dispassion in his voice was matched in his returning stare.

A man clearly used to being listened to and heeded, Gabriel Serres had a presence that commanded attention even when he wasn't speaking. Alessia had noticed him a number of times since their introduction and, though most of those times he'd been at a distance from her—apart from in the castle's private car park when she'd come close to losing her footing when their eyes had suddenly met—he'd certainly commanded *her* attention. There was something about him she found difficult to tear her gaze from, something that made her belly warm and soften even though she'd come to the conclusion that there was nothing warm or soft about him. Under the impeccably tailored grey suit lay an obviously hard, lean body that perfectly matched a hard, angular face with hooded dark brown eyes that were as warm as a frozen waterfall. Even his thick black hair had been tamed into a quiff she doubted dared escape its confines.

Anger rising that he could be so detached about a situation where a woman was required to give her entire future just to save her family's skin, Alessia eyeballed him and snapped. 'What, like Clara consented?'

'It has been agreed,' her mother said in a voice that brooked no further argument. 'Gabriel has gone to great lengths to bring a rapprochement between our nations. Your brother is in agreement, the king is in agreement and the bride is in agreement. The wedding preparations start now. The pre-wedding party will be held in two weeks, the wedding in six. You will be a bridesmaid and you will smile and show the world how happy you are for the union. We all will.' And with that, her mother rose with the innate grace only a born queen had, and swept out of the room without another look at her youngest child.

Devastated to have caused her mother such disappointment and realising she was in danger of going into a full-blown meltdown in front of her father, brother, Ice Man and the staff, Alessia got to her feet. Casting each of them a withering stare, she left the meeting room with her head as high as she could manage.

Gabriel had a tension headache, caused no doubt by three days of intense negotiations between a despotic king and a rival royal family desperately trying to salvage their own image. Having had little sleep in that period didn't help, and neither did the engine problem with his plane he'd been notified about earlier. His plan to leave the Berrutis' castle and fly home to Spain delayed, he'd accepted King Julius's offer of a bed for the night. After dining with the king and queen and the heir to the throne, he was escorted through the warren of wide corridors to his appointed quarters. Once inside, he rolled his neck and shoulders and took a shower.

As far as royal families went, the Berrutis were relatively decent. Relatively. They inhabited a privileged world where, by virtue of their births, they were exalted and deferred to from their very first breaths, and, as such, took being exalted and deferred to as their due. Compared to King Dominic Fernandes, however, they were modest paragons of virtue. Gabriel cared little either way. His job was to be impartial and broker an agreement both parties could live with and he'd done that. Negotiating a marriage was, however, a first, and had left a bad taste in his mouth, which he unsuccessfully tried to scrub out with his toothbrush. He was quite sure Princess Alessia's outrage about the marriage had contributed to the acrid taste on his tongue.

Despite his exhaustion, Gabriel was too wired to sleep. After twenty minutes of his eyes refusing to close and fighting his mind's desire to conjure the pint-sized princess, he gave up and threw the bedsheets off. Pulling on a pair of trousers, he prowled the quarters he'd been appointed, found a fully stocked bar and helped himself to a bourbon. If he wished, he could lift the receiver on the bar and call the castle kitchen, where an on-duty chef would prepare anything he desired. He would give the Berrutis their due, they were excellent hosts.

Taking the bottle of bourbon with him, he opened the French doors in his bedroom and stepped onto the balcony. The warm air of the night had lost much of the day's humidity, the distant full moon lighting the castle's extensive grounds. With a strong gothic feel, it was an intriguing castle dating back to the medieval period, and full of mysteries and secrets. In the distance he could see the ancient amphitheatre, which divided the castle's two main sections…

His thoughts cut away from him as the strong feeling of being watched made the hairs on the back of his neck rise.

Alessia had been laid in her hammock for hours. Unable to face another meal with her family, unable to bear seeing more of her mother's disappointment, unable to look at the brother whose life she'd ruined, she felt desperately alone, wracked with guilt and so very ashamed. Now, though, her heart was thumping, because a man had emerged through the shadows on the adjoining balcony, and as he turned his head in her direction her heart thumped even harder as recognition kicked in.

It was *him*. The gorgeous Ice Man who made her belly flip.

Under the moonlight, he somehow seemed even more devastatingly attractive, and she sucked in a breath as her gaze drifted over a rampantly masculine bare chest.

For a long, long moment, all the demons in her head flew away in the face of such a divine specimen of manhood.

Suddenly certain her misery had conjured him, she blinked hard to clear his image, but it didn't clear anything. That really was the gorgeous Ice Man.

Impulse took over and before she could stop herself, she called out. 'Having trouble sleeping too?'

Gabriel's heart smashed in instant recognition of the husky voice. Holding his breath, he rested an arm on the ancient waist-high stone balustrade that adjoined the neighbouring balcony, and peered into the adjoining space. There he found, laid out on a hammock in the moonlight's shadow, the woman whose unguarded words had almost caused a war between two nations and whose image had prevented him from sleeping.

He cursed silently even as his heart clattered

harder into his ribs. He'd been unaware his appointed quarters adjoined hers.

'Good evening, Your Highness,' he said politely. 'My apologies for disturbing you.'

Though her spot in the shadows prevented him from seeing her features clearly, he could feel her gaze on him.

'You're not disturbing me… Is that a bottle of scotch you're carrying?'

'Bourbon.'

'Can I have some?'

The silence that fell during his hesitation was absolute. The last thing he should encourage was a late-night conversation with the beautiful princess who'd occupied so much of his thoughts these last few days.

'Please? I could do with a drink.'

What harm could a quick drink with each remaining on their respective sides of the balcony do? He would make sure it was a quick drink. Allow her one nip and then make his excuses and return to his room. 'Of course.'

She climbed off the hammock and padded barefoot to him. As she drew closer and out of the shadows, he barely had time to register that she was wearing pretty, short pyjamas before she put her hands on the balustrade—she was so short her shoulders barely reached the top of it—and, with an effortless grace, swung herself over. In seconds she stood before him, the moonlight pouring on her casting her in an ethereal light that highlighted her delicate beauty and gave the illusion of her dark velvet eyes being limitless pools.

Spellbound, for perhaps the first time in his life, Gabriel found himself at a loss for words.

CHAPTER TWO

THERE WAS AN intensity in the princess's stare before her chest rose and she indicated the bottle engulfed in Gabriel's hand. 'May I?'

A cloud of soft, fruity scent seeped into his airwaves and darted through his senses.

Dragging himself back to the here and now, he forced a tight smile and passed it to her.

'Thanks.' She unscrewed the cap and placed it to her lips. Her small but perfectly formed mouth was one of the first things he'd noticed about her. It was like a rosebud on the cusp of blooming. She took a long drink and swallowed without so much as a flinch then delicately brushed the residue with a sweep of an elegant finger. Everything about her was elegant. Graceful.

She bestowed him with a small, sad smile that did something funny to his chest. 'May I sit?'

His next forced smile almost made his face crack. 'Of course.'

Carrying the bottle to the balcony's deep L-shaped sofa, the princess sank elegantly onto the L part and stretched her legs out, hooking her ankles together. The shorts of her pale blue pyjamas had risen to the tops of her thighs and he hastily cast his gaze down. The toes at the end of feet that were the smallest he'd ever seen on a grown woman were painted deep blue. It was a colour that complemented her golden skin and set off the delicate shapeliness of legs that appeared almost impossibly smooth.

His veins heating with dangerous awareness, Gabriel dragged his gaze from the princess's feet and looked back in her eyes...only to find himself trapped again in those beguiling orbs.

Her stare fixed on him, she took another drink of bourbon. 'Don't worry, I won't stay long,' she said softly in that husky voice. She pulled another sad smile and shrugged. 'Looks like it's true that misery loves company.'

'You are unhappy?' he asked before he could stop himself.

He shouldn't encourage conversation. The moonlight, the all-pervading silence in the air around them...it lent an intimacy to the balcony setting that made his skin tingle and heightened his senses.

'I...' She cut herself off and closed her eyes. After a mediative breath, she looked back at him, her features showing she'd composed herself. She indicated the space next to her. 'Don't stand on ceremony on my account.'

He inclined his head, thinking hard as to how to extract himself from this situation but coming up with nothing. 'You're a princess. As a commoner, I thought it was my duty to stand on ceremony.'

Her cheeks pulled into a smile fractionally wider than he'd seen from her before, and in a faintly teasing voice, she said, 'Then as a princess of this castle, I invite you to sit on the sofa of your own balcony in your own quarters.'

Alessia looked into the eyes of the man standing so rigidly he could have a pole for a spine. When he finally sat, placing himself far at the other end of the sofa, it was with the same rigidity that he'd stood.

It was nothing but a mad impulse that had made her call out to him. Nothing but a second mad impulse that had made her swing over the balustrade to his balcony. And now she was sat on his balcony sofa. Sat alone with a bare-chested man in the middle of the night where the only living beings observing them were crickets and frogs and the other nocturnal creatures who played and sang and mated when the sun went down.

'I didn't realise you'd stayed,' she said when he made no effort at conversation.

'There is a problem with my plane's engine. It should be fixed by the morning. Your parents kindly invited me to stay the night.'

'That's my parents,' she said with a muted laugh, and drank some more bourbon. 'Kindness personified.'

She saw the raising of a thick, black brow at this but his firm lips stayed closed.

Feeling a stab of disloyalty for her slight on her

parents, she changed the subject. Not that he'd allowed himself to be drawn into it. Was that discretion on his part or a lack of interest? She'd seen the way he looked at her, sensed he was attracted to her, but that didn't mean he liked her. After all, he had spent the last three days clearing up the mess she'd made. He probably thought her a vacuous troublemaker who'd brought shame on her family. The latter part was true but the former...? No. Alessia had put duty first her entire life. Maybe that's where the guilt at her disloyalty had come from—the Berrutis did not bad-mouth each other to outsiders. Their loyalty was to the monarchy as an institution first, and then to their people, and then to each other as family. 'Where are you from? I can't place your accent.'

Gabriel breathed in deeply. He wanted to ask her to return to her own quarters but was conscious that this magnificent castle was the princess's home. And conscious that she was a princess used to being deferred to. She would not take kindly to being ordered about by a commoner, and his brain ticked quickly as he tried to work out how he could extract himself from this situation without offending her. A man did not reach the heights Gabriel had in the diplomatic world by offending clients or members of their families.

Those were the reasons he tried to convince himself as to why he'd not already asked her to leave. The pulses throbbing throughout his body proved the lie. Those pulses had been throbbing since the moonlight had bathed her in its silver glow, a shimmering mirage made of flesh and blood.

Alessia Berruti was a princess, yes, but she was also a woman. A highly desirable woman.

He fisted his hands and clenched his jaw.

Alessia Berruti was a highly desirable woman he couldn't touch. Shouldn't touch. Mustn't touch.

'My mother is French, my father is Spanish,' he said in his practised even tone. 'I spent my formative years in Paris but I was raised to be bilingual.'

'You're fluent in both languages?'

'Yes.'

'And you speak Italian like a native too… Impressive.'

He didn't respond. He would not encourage this conversation. Without any encouragement, she would bore of his company and leave.

'Do you speak other languages?'

He wouldn't encourage her but it would be the height of rudeness to ignore a direct question. 'Yes.'

This was like getting blood from a stone, Alessia thought, but instead of deterring her, it only intrigued her. Most people when finding themselves in a private conversation with her fawned and flattered and set out to impress. Others became tongue-tied—it was the cloud of 'celebrity' around her that caused it—but long experience at putting those people at ease usually found them loosening up quickly. Gabriel, though, was neither of those people. He was a man who dealt with powerful people and institutions on a daily basis, and carried an air of power and authority in his own right, and everything about his body language was telling her he wanted her to leave. Which only intrigued her more. Because she'd seen that expression in his eyes which had pulsed with something quite different. 'Which ones?'

'English, German and Portuguese.'

'You're fluent in six languages? That really is impressive.'

Yet more non-response.

'Do languages come naturally to you?'

There was an almost imperceptible sigh before he answered. 'Yes.'

'I speak English fluently, but that's because I went to boarding school there,' she told him. 'I can converse in Spanish as long as it's taken at a slow pace, but my French is pretty basic, my German diabolical and I've never learned any Portuguese.'

She thought she caught a glimmer of humour on Gabriel's poker face.

'I suppose good linguistic skills are essential for your line of work,' she mused into the latest bout of silence, inordinately pleased to have made his face crack into a smile, as tepid as that smile might have been. Gabriel was so serious that she wondered if he ever truly smiled. She wondered if he ever allowed himself to. He was the most intriguing person she'd met in a long, long time. Maybe ever.

'Yes.'

'And what made you choose diplomacy as a career? I don't imagine it came up on a list of career choices when you were at school.'

Another quickly vanishing glimmer of humour.

'I learned at a young age that I had an aptitude for diplomacy.'

'Who discovers something like that?'

'I did.'

'How?'

Those dreamy light brown eyes suddenly fixed on her. A charge laced her spine, even stronger than the shiver she'd experienced when gazing at him earlier. 'Forgive me, Your Highness, but that is personal.'

The sudden flash of steel she caught told her his wish for forgiveness was pure lip service. He was giving her a diplomatic answer that translated into *mind your own business*.

Another charge thrummed through her. This man was no sycophant. This man had a core of steel. That self-containment, coupled with his drop-dead gorgeous looks and tripled with the innate self-confidence that oozed from his bronzed skin, made him the sexiest man she'd ever laid eyes on.

'That's perfectly reasonable,' she assured him although she was perfectly certain he didn't want or care for her assurance. 'And please, call me Alessia.'

His jaw tightened but he inclined his head in acknowledgement.

She took another drink of the bourbon, allowing herself a glance over the sculpturally perfect chest she found so fascinating. The moonlight had turned the bronze silver, and if not for the dark hair covering so much of the chest and forearms, she could believe he'd been cast in it.

'Where do you live?' she asked, passing the bottle to him. 'If that's not considered too personal a question.'

She noticed he made sure not to allow their fingers to touch as he took it from her.

'I travel a lot with my work.' He poured a small measure into a glass she hadn't even noticed him holding.

'I'd already gathered that, but you must have a place you call home.'

She noticed his jaw clenching. 'I consider Spain to be my home.'

'Which part?'

'Madrid.'

'I've visited Madrid many times. It's a beautiful city.'

He took a large sip of the bourbon and swirled it in his mouth a long time before swallowing. His throat was as sculpturally perfect as the rest of him.

'You don't like me, do you?' she said after another bout of lengthy silence.

That strong, perfect throat moved before he answered. 'What makes you think that?'

'Just a feeling. And you didn't deny it.'

'I cannot help how you feel.' He drank the rest of his bourbon.

'Do you blame me for the mess between my family and Dominic?'

'It is not my place to cast blame.' He poured himself another measure. 'My role is only to find solutions all parties can live with.'

'Your role doesn't prevent you forming opinions.'

'It prevents me voicing them.' He extended the bottle to her.

Her fingers brushed against his as she took it from him. The electric shock that flew through her skin was so strong that her eyes widened at the same moment Gabriel yanked his hand back as if he too had felt the burn. It took her a beat to find her voice again. 'So you do have opinions?'

'Everyone has opinions. Not everyone has the sense to know when those opinions should not be voiced.'

'Like when I voiced my opinion on Dominic?'

An extremely thick black eyebrow rose but his answer was a diplomatic, 'If people only voiced their opinions at appropriate times, I would be out of a job.'

She considered this with a small laugh. 'Then you should be grateful to me…' She winced and shook her head. 'Forget I said that. It was crass of me.' She sighed. 'And I owe you an apology too, for the way I spoke to you earlier. My tone was rude. I apologise.'

There was a detectable softening in his stare and in his voice too when he said, 'You were upset.'

'There is never an excuse for rudeness.'

'But there is often a reason for it,' he countered with the ghost of a smile and a glint in his eye that said far more than would come from his mouth, and she realised that he understood.

To Alessia's horror, hot tears welled up. She didn't want to cry. She had no idea why but the last thing she wanted was to appear weak and fragile in Gabriel's eyes. She suspected he had no time for weak and fragile women. She *wasn't* a weak and fragile woman. She wasn't. Not normally. Tiny but Mighty, her brother Marcelo used to call her. But Marcelo wasn't there: the one member of her family she could usually rely on for support was abroad on his honeymoon, and she'd had to suffer days of everyone else's anger and disapproval without any respite, so to have this man of all people offer her a crumb of comfort… It only made all the guilt and anguish she'd been suffering, which had diminished in the excitement of Gabriel's appearance, rise back to the surface.

A tear rolled down her cheek. She wiped it away and tried desperately to compose herself. In that moment it felt like one more blow could shatter her to pieces. 'I just feel so responsible about everything. Not just Amadeo's marriage but everything.'

He gazed at her for the longest time, piercingly intense eyes slightly narrowed, his mouth a straight line, as if he were weighing whether to speak what was on his mind. And then he closed his eyes briefly and inhaled. When his eyes snapped back on hers, he leaned a little closer and said in a low timbre, 'What you said at your brother's wedding was just one piece of a large jigsaw of enmity between your nation and Dominic's. You were not responsible for anything that occurred beforehand. The structural damage between the two nations had already been done.'

Alessia had no idea why this attempt at reassurance made her feel worse, but the tears she'd been fighting burst free and tumbled down her face like a waterfall before she could do anything to stop them.

With a sharp tightening in his chest and guts, Gabriel closed his eyes to the sobbing princess.

His sister had been a master at turning on the tears, using them as a weapon to manipulate their warring parents in her favour. He'd rather admired her for it. Since he'd left home, though, the women he'd chosen to acquaint himself with were women like himself: reserved, stoical and never prone to histrionics. As a result, he had no idea how he was supposed to handle this situation. He couldn't throw money or the promise of clothes or the promise of a specially wanted treat at Alessia as his parents had done when Mariella turned on the waterworks. So, when he opened his eyes and found her knees brought to her chest and her face buried in them, one hand still clinging tightly to the bottle of bourbon, he did the one thing he really didn't want to do, and moved closer to her.

First removing the bottle and placing it on the floor, he then patted her heaving shoulders in what he hoped was a reassuring manner. To his consternation, she twisted into him. A slender arm snaked around his waist, and then she sagged against him and wept into his chest.

'I'm sorry,' she sobbed. 'I don't want to cry but I just feel so bad. One unthinking comment and now Amadeo has to marry a stranger and an unwilling woman is being forced into marriage with him, and it's all my fault.'

Gabriel closed his eyes again and gritted his teeth, trying to block out the sensory overload of having this most beautiful of women crying in his arms. It had been a battle he'd fought since Alessia had joined him, uninvited, on his balcony.

He'd never been in a situation like this before. For sure, there had been women who'd invited themselves into his space through the years—the foreign minister of a Scandinavian country who'd turned up at the door of his hotel room with a bottle of Dom Pérignon came to mind—and he'd been able to disentangle himself from those potentially dangerous situations with no harm done and no hurt feelings. The difference, he knew, was that he'd not been attracted to any of those women. Gabriel was select in his choice of lovers. A celebrity princess who also happened to be a close family member of an existing client—the very reason for his being employed by that client— was as far removed as a choice of lover as he would ever make, and yet there wasn't a cell in his body that hadn't attuned itself to her since she'd called out to him from the shadows in that sexy, husky voice.

The rack of her distress, though, wove through his veins to penetrate his heart, and the instinct to comfort overrode the last of his self-preservation. Gabriel wrapped an arm around her and held her tightly to him.

Dios, his heart was thumping.

Nothing was said for the longest time as, slowly, Alessia's sobs subsided.

He could feel the heat of her breath against the dampness of her tears on his naked chest.

Swallowing hard, knowing that with every second that passed with his arms around her he was dancing with danger, Gabriel rested his chin on her head and quietly said, 'I know you're concerned for Amadeo's bride, but I assure you, she is willing.'

'How can you know that?' She squeezed her arm even tighter around him, her husky voice muffled. 'Dominic doesn't believe in giving women choices. He held Clara against her will and would have forced her down the aisle if Marcelo hadn't rescued her.'

'I know because I spoke to Elsbeth privately to satisfy myself that she was a willing participant. I do have principles and there is no sum of money on earth that would see me be party to a forced marriage.'

Slowly, the princess lifted her face and gazed into his eyes. 'How can you be so sure? Dominic might have forced her to lie. He might have guessed that you would want to speak with her privately.'

It was staring into those dark, velvet orbs that made it a sudden effort to speak and filled his veins with lava. Just unimaginable depths...

He had to clear his throat to speak. 'The eyes don't lie, Princess. You have to take my word that her eyes showed only excitement. She's glad to be leaving Monte Cleure.'

And his loins were trying to show *their* excitement. They were responding to the princess being pressed so tightly against him, the feel of her small breasts jutting into his naked chest... The telltale tug of arousal battled for supremacy against his willpower and, for the first time in decades, it was winning.

Her brow furrowed. 'Excitement?' she asked doubtfully.

He needed to extract himself from this situation right now. To stay like this would be madness. *Was* madness.

'Think about it,' he murmured roughly, clenching the silk of her pyjama vest top to stop himself from slipping a hand beneath it. 'Why did your family refuse to entertain the notion of you marrying Dominic, even before he kidnapped Clara?'

Understanding glimmered in the warm depths of her brown eyes. 'Because he's a monster,' she whispered.

Unwilling to incriminate himself verbally, Gabriel inclined his head and, for no good reason, inched his face closer to hers. Now he could smell the underlying scent of the princess's skin beneath the soft fruitiness. It was intoxicating. As intoxicating as the sight of those pretty rosebud lips barely inches from his own. 'Now put yourself in her shoes,' he said, his voice so low even he struggled to hear it. 'If you were a member of the Fernandes royal family living under Dominic's rule and the opportunity came for you to marry into another royal family with a more…' So many heady feelings were shooting and weaving through him that he had to grope for the word. '*Benign* reputation, what would you do?'

Dominic's rule over his people was absolute. His rule over his family, especially the female members, was a clenched iron glove.

And this woman, this sexy, beautiful, fragile woman, had wanted to marry him to right the wrong of the mess she'd created.

He could never have been party to negotiations in

which Alessia had been the pawn, he realised hazily, soaking in every delicate feature of her face. Not even if she'd been a willing pawn as Amadeo's bride was.

Alessia had become so spellbound by Gabriel's eyes that his words had dissolved into nothing but a caress to her senses. She'd thought he had brown eyes like her own but the irises were so transparent that, this close, it was like looking into golden supernovas ringing around pulsating black holes.

To think she'd thought his eyes cold when they contained such life and colour and fired such warmth that their radiation was heating her insides in a way she'd never felt before. Or was it the warmth of his hard body heating her veins and melting her deep in the secret place no man had touched before?

She supposed she should move her arm from around his waist but right then his solid comfort and the warmth of his flesh seeping through the thin fabric of her pyjamas made her reluctant to do what propriety said she should do.

She'd never been held by a man like this before.

Still staring into his eyes, she whispered, 'I'm sorry for making a scene.'

A finger dragged gently along her cheekbone. 'You haven't.'

She shivered and pressed herself closer.

He was divine, she thought dimly, from the thick black eyebrows to the long straight nose to the angular jaw that had been clean shaven only hours before but was now covered in thick black stubble. That stubble carried on down to his strong neck until it tapered away leaving bronzed skin so smooth that her hand tugged itself from its hold around his back to skim lightly up the hard planes of his chest to gently palm his throat and feel the smoothness for herself.

If someone had told Gabriel that morning that he would end the day in the battle of his life, he would have laughed disdainfully, but now, trapped in the seductive gaze of this incredibly sexy and enthrallingly beautiful woman, the darts of arousal he'd been fighting had turned into flames and his efforts to remember all the reasons he needed to resist these feelings for her were fading. Thoughts themselves had become ephemeral clouds, and when the elegant fingers stroked his neck at the same moment the rosebud lips parted, a jolt of electricity struck that vanquished the clouds leaving only the man in his rawest form.

CHAPTER THREE

ALESSIA HAD BEEN kissed only once. It had been at the leaving ball at her English boarding school at which sixth formers from the twinned boy's school nearby had been invited. Drinks had been spiked and inhibitions, which a born princess like Alessia had in spades, were dismantled. What she remembered most about that kiss was its slobberiness. In the five years that had passed, she'd looked back on that night with a certain wistfulness. If she'd known it would be her only kiss she would have made the most of it, slobberiness or not. It wasn't that Alessia prized her virginity, more that she was acutely aware of her position and that the eyes of the world followed her whenever she left the castle grounds. Many of the eligible men she came across were either sycophants or leeches or brimming with pomposity. Often all three. If she was to be linked to a man, the press would make a huge deal about it, and if she was to put herself under what would be an even greater microscope than the one dealt with on a daily basis then that man needed to be worth it. She wanted to respect the man she gave her heart to, and be confident that he wouldn't sell stories about her or her family. No such man had come into her life.

When Gabriel's firm mouth found hers, the feelings that engulfed her were so incredible that it made her five-year kissing abstinence worthwhile.

Now *this* was a kiss…

Alessia closed her eyes and sank into the headiness of a mouth that sent sensation thrumming through her lips and over her skin and then seeped beneath the flesh to awaken every cell in her body.

Wrapping her arms tightly around his neck, her hunger unleashed and she returned the kiss with all the passion that had hidden dormant for so long inside her. At the first stroke of his tongue against hers, the heat that filled her insides was strong enough to melt bone, and when his hands roamed the planes of her back there was only a dim shock that she had, at some point since their mouths found each other, shifted her body so that she was straddling his lap.

She didn't want to think, she thought dreamily as his mouth broke from hers and dipped down to the sensitive skin of her neck and his hands lifted her silk pyjama vest top up and over her head. If a touch and a kiss could evoke such wonderful pleasure then she wanted to fall into it.

For the first time in her life, she wanted to forget who she was and all the expectations she put on herself for being Princess Alessia, and let all the demons be thrown aside and just *feel*, because she'd had no idea that feeling could be so incredible.

A voice in her head whispered that she should tell Gabriel she was a virgin…

She pushed the voice away.

The moment the pyjama top was discarded, Gabriel cupped her cheeks tightly and kissed her with an ardency that sent more incredible tingles racing through her. Alessia dove her fingers through the thick black hair and moaned when his mouth assaulted her neck again, gladly letting his hands manipulate her into arching her back so he could take one of her breasts into his mouth. At the first flicker of his tongue against her erect nipple, she gasped at the thrill of pleasure, and dug her fingers even harder against his skull, and when she shifted slightly and felt the hard wedge pressing against the apex of her thighs, instinct had her press down and gasp even louder at the pulsing sensations that enflamed her.

Gabriel's arousal was such that when Alessia ground down on him, the barrier of thin clothing separating them was barrier enough to make a grown man weep for release. No woman's skin had ever tasted this good or felt this soft, Gabriel thought as he devoured Alessia's other breast. And what beautiful breasts they were, tiny and high and with dark tips as moreish as her rosebud lips.

He didn't know who was more desperate for him to take possession of her. Alessia ground down on him, cradling his head tightly against her breasts, and when she gave another of the throaty moans that added fuel to his arousal, all he could focus on was his need to be inside her. In an instant, he flipped her round so she was on her back. In an instant, her legs wrapped around his waist and she was grabbing at his buttocks, rosebud mouth finding his and kissing him with the hot sweetness that was as intoxicating as everything else about her. Mouths fused, hands grabbed down low, brushing against each other as they scrambled to undo his trousers and rid Alessia of her pyjama shorts. Without breaking the connection of their mouths, they managed to rid themselves of her shorts and then Gabriel was free from his own confines and Alessia was using her toes to yank them down to his knees. Any idea of kicking his trousers off were forgotten when she arched up with her pelvis and he felt her slickness.

Damn but she was as hot and ready for him as he was for her.

Her hands grabbed his buttocks again, and that was it for him. Spreading her thighs and pushing them up, he thrust deep into the tight, tight heat.

The discomfort was so momentary that Alessia ignored it. How could she do anything else when she was being filled so gloriously and completely?

She'd watched enough sex scenes to know what to expect but this was so much more than she could ever have known and she cried out with every hard drive inside her, Gabriel's each and every thrust filling her so greatly that her mind detached itself from her body and she became nothing but a vessel of sensual ecstasy.

Breathless groans and cries of pleasure mingled

between their enjoined mouths, fingers bit into flesh and scraped through hair, the moans between them intensifying as something deep inside her wound tightly, coiling and coiling, *burning*.

Gabriel, lost in a hedonistic cloud, resisted the demand for release building inside him. Never, in all his thirty-five years on this earth, had he experienced anything like this, such complete sensory capitulation. It wasn't just the feel of being inside Alessia's tightness—and Lord, such unbelievable tightness—it was the feel of her flesh compressed so tightly to his, the seductively sweet taste of her mouth, the scent of their coupling… It was mind-blowing, and he didn't want it to end. He spread her thighs even further to reach even deeper penetration—Lord, this was something else—and lifted his face from hers so he could stare at the face of the woman as beautiful as the body he was pounding into, and when he plunged his tongue into her mouth again and heard the throaty groan as she thickened around him, he could hold on no more and, with a roar of ecstasy, Gabriel let go.

Gabriel quietly donned his clothes using the small stream of dusky light through the gap in his curtains to see by. The sun was rising. Soon it would be day. Soon the castle would come to life. He wanted to be gone before that happened.

Before he left, he gazed at the dark hair poking out above the bedsheets, the figure the hair belonged to huddled beneath. His heart clenched into a fist.

He'd never experienced a night like that before.

He'd never lost himself like that before. He'd been cast under a spell, that was the only explanation for it. He usually came right back to himself after sex but with Alessia the spell had remained intact. He'd carried her delectable body to his bedroom and made love to her again. The second time, they'd taken it much slower, the combustible lust that had exploded between them reduced to a simmer that had seen them exploring each other's bodies until every inch had been discovered and worshipped. His climax had been every bit as powerful as the first time. They'd finally fallen into slumber hours after the rest of Ceres had gone to sleep. And then he'd woken up and the spell had been lifted.

All he wanted now was to leave before Alessia stirred. Self-recriminations about bedding a client's family member—a princess, no less—could wait until he was in the privacy of his own home.

She stirred beneath the sheets. He held his breath as a throb of desire stirred in his loins and closed his eyes tightly. He would not return to that bed, however deep his craving.

Only when satisfied that she was still safely asleep did he slip out of the room.

Not wishing to see any member of the Berruti family, uncertain he'd be able to look any of them in the eye, he called the driver he'd been appointed, left a note for Queen Isabella, King Julius and Prince Amadeo thanking them for their hospitality and, ten minutes later, left the castle grounds.

* * *

For the first time in Alessia's life, she didn't fight waking up. Even before her eyes opened, she thrilled to be awake, the magic of the previous night flashing through her.

For the first time in her life, Alessia had thrown propriety, duty and decorum to the wind and allowed the woman beneath the princess skin to take control. It had been sublime. If she closed her eyes she could still feel the echo of the fulfilment throbbing deep between her legs.

Joy filled her and she laughed softly as she opened her eyes, fully expecting to find Gabriel's gorgeous face on the pillow beside hers.

His side of the bed was empty.

Holding the bedsheets to her naked form, she sat up. 'Gabriel?'

No response.

Climbing out of bed, she quickly yanked her pyjama bottoms off the floor—when had *they* been brought in from the balcony?—and pulled them on and padded to the bathroom. She knocked on the door. No answer. A quick look behind the door found it empty.

Slipping the pyjama vest top over her head and, trying hard to fight against the coldness filling her veins, Alessia left the bedroom calling out his name again.

The guest quarters Gabriel had been appointed, usually given to family members like her parents' siblings, were nearly a mirror image of her own. Laid out like an apartment, it had a bedroom and adjoining bathroom, a guest room with its own bathroom, a dayroom, a dining room, a reception room and an unused kitchen. Gabriel was nowhere to be seen. Nor were his clothes.

The quarters being on the second floor, a set of iron steps ran off the balcony and led down to the private gardens. She hurried down the steps barefoot.

Although brimming with early-morning birdsong, the garden was empty of human life.

Her heart thumping, she checked each room of his quarters a second time and then a third, her calls of his name gradually weakening to a choked whisper. Back in the bedroom, she stared at the bed. It was the very first time she'd shared a bed with another human being. She could still smell Gabriel. Could still feel his touch on her skin.

In a daze, she stepped back onto the balcony and stared at the plump sofa she'd lost her virginity on. Limbs now feeling all watery, she somehow managed to climb over the balustrade and back onto her private abode. Inside, she called the family's head of housekeeping, not even bothering to think of an excuse to explain why she was enquiring about the whereabouts of the negotiator who'd saved the Berrutis from almost certain destruction.

The answer, although expected, still landed as a blow.

Gabriel had gone.

He hadn't even left her a note of goodbye.

* * *

Alessia closed her eyes and resisted pulling at her just-done hair. She felt sick. After a few minutes spent doing breathing exercises, she felt no better, and briefly considered calling her mother and telling her she felt too ill to attend Amadeo and Elsbeth's pre-wedding party.

She couldn't miss the party. A royal princess did not bow out of engagements from something as pathetic as illness, not unless she was at death's door, which a bout of nausea did not class as. Not that it was a royal engagement as the public would recognise it. As far as the public were concerned, the party was a private affair although the carefully selected members of the press corps who'd be in attendance to document the evening—and it was a momentous occasion and not just because the heir to the throne would be showing off his new bride-to-be—would publish the usual photos and video clips to allow the public to feel a part of the event. So, a private event with as much privacy as the animals in London Zoo had. And Alessia had to smile and dance with that horrible monster King Dominic Fernandez of Monte Cleure to prove to the world that there was no bad feeling between them. She'd bet that was the cause of her nausea.

There was a knock on her bedroom door.

Opening her eyes, she stared at her reflection and brought her practised smile to her face before calling out, 'Come in.'

Rather than a member of her domestic staff, her

visitor was her new sister-in-law. Immediately, Alessia's spirits lifted. Clara was the woman Marcelo had rescued from King Dominic's evil clutches. It was that rescue, photographed and leaked to the world, which had started the diplomatic war between the two countries. The fallout from the rescue had compelled Marcelo to marry Clara himself and, as a result, Alessia had a brand-new sister-in-law. What made it even better was that Marcelo and Clara had fallen madly in love for real.

There was an acute pang in her chest as Alessia wondered if a man would ever look at her the way Marcelo looked at Clara, a pang made sharper as Gabriel Serres's handsome face floated in her eyes. She willed the image away.

She'd not heard even a whisper from him since he'd snuck out of the bed they'd made love in.

For days she'd drifted around the palace in a fugue of disbelief. Disbelief that she'd fallen head over heels in lust with a man she barely knew, falling so hard and so fast that she'd given her virginity without any thought, too wrapped up in the moment to care about anything but the wonder of what they were sharing. Disbelief that Gabriel had left without a word of goodbye when they'd shared such an incredible night together. Disbelief at Gabriel's subsequent silence.

And then she'd made the fatal mistake of making excuses for his silence. After three days of this fugue-like drifting, she'd convinced herself an emergency had taken him from their bed and that he'd left without waking her because he wanted her to have more sleep. She'd convinced herself too that the only reason he hadn't called was because he didn't have her personal number and that to ask her brother or parents or any of their staff for it would lead to too many questions. Gabriel was experienced enough in her world to know a man didn't just casually ask for a princess's personal number. And so she'd decided to put them both out of their misery—because *surely* he was in as big a flux as she was after what they'd shared—and call him, asking her private secretary to obtain his number for her.

It was a business number answered by an efficient-sounding woman. Alessia left a message. For days she'd waited on tenterhooks, her heart leaping every time her phone buzzed. There had been no call back.

Her pride wouldn't let her ask her secretary to go one further and obtain his personal number, and even if it wasn't out of the question for Alessia to obtain it from her parents or brother, she finally opened her eyes and let reality sink in. It simply wasn't possible that Gabriel's assistant hadn't passed the message on. Gabriel had simply ignored it.

He'd deliberately crept out of their bed without waking her.

He hadn't called her because he didn't want to.

Despite everything they'd shared, he didn't want to see her again and didn't think her worthy of a two-minute call to tell her this.

Alessia had given her virginity to a man who was treating her like a worthless one-night stand. Now, just over two weeks on, she was well and truly done with hoping and moping.

Gabriel Serres could go to hell.

'Hi, sis,' Clara said chirpily, bounding over to the dressing table and bringing out the first smile on Alessia's face in two weeks. 'You look fantastic! That dress is amazing! Gosh, I am so envious.'

'You can talk,' Alessia laughed, rising from her seat to embrace her tightly. Where she had chosen an elegant deep red strapless ballgown for the party, Clara had gone for a toga-style shimmering silver dress that accentuated the bust Alessia would give her left kidney for. 'You look beautiful.'

Clara beamed. 'Thank you. Call me petty but I really want to look my best tonight for King Pig. Rub his face in it a bit more.'

'You're not worried about seeing him?'

'If anyone should be worried, it's *him*. Marcelo has promised Amadeo not to make a scene and I think it's going to kill him to keep that promise. I have to keep reminding him that he got his revenge on the monster when he rescued me from him.'

'Did Amadeo make you promise not to cause a scene too?'

'I promised that voluntarily. After all, I'm trying to be the perfect princess and the perfect princess doesn't karate chop guests at a grand social function, does she?' She actually looked a touch woebegone at not being able to do this.

Alessia giggled then changed the subject. 'How did the honeymoon go?' This was the first time the two old friends had had a chance for a private catch-up since Clara and Marcelo's return from their honeymoon. 'Were the Seychelles as pretty as you hoped?'

'It was amazing! Not that we saw all that much of it as we spent most of our time in bed—'

'Hold it right there,' she interrupted before Clara could start giving details. 'I'm feeling sick enough as it is without having to listen to details about my brother's sex life.'

Clara cackled but then her brow furrowed. 'You're feeling sick? What's wrong?'

'I've just been feeling a bit off for a couple of days. Probably something I ate.'

She looked even more closely at her. 'Any other symptoms?'

'No.'

But Clara continued to scrutinise her. 'Are you wearing a padded bra?'

'I'm not wearing a bra. Why?'

'Your boobs have grown. If I didn't know better, I'd ask if you were pregnant.'

Those words set off an instantaneous reaction in Alessia. Cold white noise filled her head, cold dread prickled her skin. Instinctively, she put her hand to her abdomen and breathed hard.

'Alessia? Are you okay? Your face has gone a funny colour.'

But Clara's voice had become distant and Alessia had to lean into her dressing table to support her weak frame as the room began to spin wildly around her.

* * *

Gabriel dispassionately watched the previous evening's footage of Prince Amadeo and Lady Elsbeth's pre-wedding party in his hotel room in Rome. Italy, a country that shared a language and much cultural history with Ceres, was enthralled by the wedding between the glamorous heir to the throne and his pretty bride-to-be. The breakfast television channel he was watching as he prepared for the day's meetings with his newest client had so far devoted over two minutes to it.

He'd been invited to the party but politely declined. He had no wish to be part of a montage such as the one being televised.

His stomach clenched when the footage came to its star turn, the attendee its viewers would have been waiting for a glimpse of above all others: Europe's premiere princess, Princess Alessia. The clenching sharpened as he watched her laughing with a member of the British royal family before the camera cut to her dancing with the King of Monte Cleure. The smile on her face belied what he knew would be crawling beneath her skin to be held in the arms of a man she so despised, and Gabriel felt a stab of anger at her family for forcing this dance on her.

'I think we can safely agree that the animosity between these two nations is now a thing of the past,' a gushing reporter was saying as the cameras panned back to the studio.

Gabriel turned the television off and pinched the bridge of his nose.

A trade and diplomatic war had been averted. Any popular uprising against their royal family from the Ceresian people, who would surely have blamed them if the situation had deteriorated further and hit them economically, had been avoided. Dominic felt valued as a 'player' again. Everyone was happy.

This should be a moment of quiet satisfaction at a job well done but the discontent at seeing Alessia again was too strong. Truth was, Gabriel was furious with himself for what had happened between them and time had not abated that fury an iota. He'd had a few one-night stands over the years—he wasn't a saint—but this was the only one he truly regretted. And the only one he couldn't erase from his head.

Couldn't erase *her* from his head. He still felt the weight of his arousal for her as a memory in his loins.

He still had her number in his wallet from when she'd called the business line. His heart had thumped so hard when his PA passed Alessia's message to him that he wouldn't have been surprised if it had smashed straight through his ribcage.

The message had been brief, inviting him to call her if he wished. He'd read it a number of times, his heart deflating as the meaning had become clear.

Alessia wanted to see him again.

It was out of the question.

He should have called her back and politely made his excuses.

What he should have done before that was say goodbye and explain that as great as their night together had been, it was a one-night-only thing.

What he should have done before any of those things was rewind even further and not sleep with her in the first place.

But he should have called her back.

He'd never treated a woman so callously before. But then, he'd never reacted so strongly to a woman before or felt such a strong reaction towards him from a woman before. Or lost his mind the way he had with her.

Despite everything, he removed the folded Post-it note from his wallet and stared at the number he'd committed to memory at the first reading. It was the strength of his desire to call her back that had stopped him doing just that. Look at him now— twenty seconds of footage of her had distracted him from his preparations as effectively as a tornado hitting his hotel room.

Alessia Berruti was a princess. She was Europe's most photographed woman. She was the antithesis of what he wanted in a partner. Gabriel's childhood had been destroyed by press intrusion and he had no wish to experience the media spotlight again under any circumstance. It would be a disaster for his career too—anonymity was essential for him to be effective. Even a casual affair with the princess who seemingly loved the spotlight would bring press intrusion of unimaginable levels.

As scalding…as *fantastic*…as their lovemaking had been, he could never see or speak to Alessia Berruti again.

He had to forget her.

Another burst of unwelcome fury raged through him and he crushed the note into a tight ball. Before he could throw it in the bin—maybe burn it to ash first for good measure—his phone rang.

He gritted his teeth and took a deep breath before reaching for it. Anger was the most futile of emotions, one he rarely succumbed to. He'd suffered more of it these last two weeks than he had the whole of his life and needed to rid himself of it.

His heart managed to jolt and sink at the same time when Prince Amadeo's name flashed on the screen.

'Good morning, Your Highness,' he said smoothly, refusing to allow a trace of his emotions show in his voice. 'This is an unexpected pleasure. What can I do for you?'

'You can explain to me how the—' an expletive was shot into Gabriel's ear '—you managed to get my sister pregnant.'

CHAPTER FOUR

'How do I look?' Alessia asked as she checked her reflection one last time. She'd selected a pair of deep blue fitted trousers, a simple short-sleeved, high-necked silk top a shade lighter, and a thick satin band separating the two items around her waist. After much deliberation, she'd left her hair loose. She'd originally tied it into a severe bun but Clara had said it made it look like she was trying too hard. According to Clara, the bun sent the message of 'this is me *proving* that seeing you again doesn't affect me in the slightest,' instead of the 'seeing you doesn't affect me in the slightest' look Alessia was aiming for.

Clara looked her up and down and nodded approvingly. 'Perfect.'

Alessia swallowed. Her world had been thrown into chaos but she could always rely on her sister-in-law's honesty. Clara's 'perfect' answer meant Alessia had achieved what she set out to. To get through the meeting that would bring her face to face with the man who'd slipped out of her life without a goodbye and which would determine the rest of her life, she needed to look as perfect on the outside as she could. God knew she was a shambles inside.

It was Clara's comment that she could believe Alessia to be pregnant that had started it all. Alessia must have had her head in the sand because until that point, she hadn't put together the dots of a late period, tender breasts and nausea. Until that point, she hadn't registered that she had no memory of Gabriel using contraception.

What fateful naivety. What brainless stupidity.

She still had no idea how she'd got through Amadeo's party. If Clara hadn't stayed so close throughout the evening, she probably wouldn't have. Clara had come to the rescue when it came to the pregnancy test too. Knowing how difficult it would be for Alessia to buy one without detection, she'd popped to a pharmacist the next morning with her security detail. Let them think the test was for her! she'd said. She'd then sneaked it over to Alessia and sat holding her hand while they waited for the result to show, and hugged her and stroked her hair for an hour while Alessia sobbed over the positive result. Unfortunately, Clara was incapable of telling a lie, and when she'd returned to her quarters and Marcelo asked what she and Alessia had been doing, she'd felt compelled to tell him the truth. Even more unfortunately, their father happened to be there too.

There had been no time at all for Alessia to come to terms with her situation before her whole family and the majority of the palace staff knew about the pregnancy. Within two hours of the positive result an emergency family meeting was convened. For the second time in less than a month, Alessia was the subject behind said meeting.

Barely a day had passed since that positive result and she still hadn't fully come to terms with it, not on an emotional level. Her family had gone straight to damage limitation mode and she'd been carried by the panicking swell with them.

If she'd thought her mother's disappointment at her unguarded comment about Dominic had hurt, it had nothing on the cold anger she'd been hit with over the pregnancy, wounding far more deeply than Amadeo's furious diatribe.

She checked her eyes one last time to ensure the drops she'd put in them that magically disappeared redness from all the crying she'd done were still working, then slipped her feet into a pair of silver heels, dabbed some perfume to her neck and wrists and left her quarters.

If not for a lifetime of poise, just one of the many things drilled into her from the moment she could walk, her first glimpse of Gabriel in the meeting room of her mother's private offices would have knocked her off her feet. Her heart thumped so hard she couldn't breathe but she kept her back straight and her head high and strolled with all the nonchalance in the world to the empty chair.

Whatever happened in this meeting, her eyes would stay dry. She was a princess and she would remember her breeding and remain regal if it killed her.

Above all else, she would not let Gabriel know that

seeing him again made her feel more violently sick than any pregnancy sickness.

She'd been nothing but a night of fun for him, quickly discarded and even more quickly forgotten.

It would be too humiliating if he guessed how deeply their night together had affected her. She could still feel the whisper of his touch on her skin. Still caught phantom whiffs of his cologne. Still felt her insides clench to remember how wonderful his lovemaking had been.

A member of staff held the chair out for her and she sat with a nod of thanks and cast her gaze around every person sat at the large oval table. Her family— her parents and two brothers, who Alessia was sandwiched between—and the family lawyer, sat at one end. At the other end sat Gabriel and a woman she assumed was his lawyer. The only person her eyes skimmed over rather than meeting their stare head-on was Gabriel. She'd intended to but at the very last second been unable to go through with it. She didn't think she could bear to see the expression in his eyes.

Skimming her eyes didn't stop the blood pumping through her body as she still somehow managed to soak in every last detail about him, from the impossibly uncreased white shirt he wore to the perfectly positioned quiff of the black hair she'd thrilled to run her fingers through.

Jutting her chin, she rested her hands flat on the table, praying no one could see the tremor in them, and purposefully faced Amadeo. Channelling their long-dead grandmother, who'd taken regal haughtiness to heights that deserved to be acknowledged as an art, she said, 'Has he agreed to accept his responsibility?'

Gabriel had watched Alessia make her grand entrance with his heart in his mouth.

Feelings he couldn't begin to describe had clawed and fisted his guts and heart since Amadeo's bombshell. When he'd driven through the castle gates, the usual photographers on duty hoping to get a shot of a Berruti family member or newsworthy associate bound for disappointment by his blacked-out windows, the clawing and fisting had reached a pinnacle. Damn it, unless he treaded very carefully, this would be his life again.

The woman he'd never wanted to see again was pregnant with his child, and it enraged him that the blame for it was going to be laid on his shoulders by Alessia as well as her family. He'd thought better of her.

He'd thought better of himself too. But they'd both been there. They'd both got carried away and failed to use protection. After their first failure there had been little point in bothering with it, and truth was, the first time had been so damn glorious that he'd wanted to experience every single aspect of it again. Maybe that's why it had felt so good, he thought darkly. That was the first time he'd made love without a barrier. He was clean. He'd assumed the princess was too, something else that weighed on his mind—since when did he give the benefit of the doubt to anyone about anything, especially with regards to his sexual health?

Keeping himself safe, aka Contraception, was his responsibility. This had the added benefit of him never having to worry that there might be miniature Gabriel Serres roaming the earth, and, as all these thoughts flashed through his mind, he found himself wondering if this had been her plan all along, to seduce him and get impregnated by him. Because she sure as hell hadn't mentioned that she wasn't on the pill. He could forgive the first time they'd made love—the madness had trapped them both—but allowing him to make love to her a second time knowing there was nothing to stop an accidental conception? Not taking action to stop any conception when there *was* still time? Unforgiveable.

Intentional or accidental, he was there, about to negotiate for his life and the life of his unborn child. He could play hardball and insist they wait until the birth for a DNA test but knew it would do nothing but delay the inevitable. He knew in his heart the child was his, but if Alessia wanted him to go along with her family's demands then she'd damned well better start showing him some respect or he would walk out of there and make the whole damn family wait until the birth for fresh negotiations.

He exhaled the anger that had spiked through him at Alessia's contemptuous tone as well as her unjustified blame. He would not allow *any* emotion to show. He needed to treat this like every negotiation he'd taken control of since he was a teenage boy negotiating his warring parents' divorce.

'I am more than willing to accept responsibility,'

he informed the side of her head icily, before her brother could speak. 'The extent of that responsibility is still to be decided, but whatever the outcome of these negotiations, I will support my child and be a father to it.'

'What is there to negotiate?' Marcelo asked, his eyes blazing. 'You've got my sister pregnant. You have to marry her.'

Gabriel folded his arms across his chest. 'Actually, I don't.'

'You took advantage of her,' Amadeo spat.

'I took advantage of a twenty-three-year-old woman?' he drawled with a hint of disdain.

Angry colour stained the heir's cheeks. He would have said something else had Queen Isabella not placed her hand lightly on his. 'You have to see things from our position,' she said.

'I do,' Gabriel countered, 'and as I understand it, you fear news of the princess's pregnancy will cause a scandal in your country which, coming so close to the recent scandals, will dent your already waning popularity and lead to more voices joining the chorus for Ceres to become a republic. Is that the measure of it?'

Barely a flicker of emotion crossed the monarch's face. 'Yes.'

'Then allow me to state my position. I will marry your daughter, and I will marry her for one reason only—to enable my child to be raised with a parent who prioritises their emotional wellbeing rather than leave them to the mercy of a family who cares more about duty and public perception than what's best for them.'

There was a sharp intake of breath from every member of the royal family. With the exception of Alessia, who didn't react at all.

He failed to understand why they should be shocked at his observation. After all, Amadeo was marrying to salvage the public's perception of the Berrutis and head off talks of republicanism. Marcelo, however happy his marriage appeared to be, had married for the same reason. And now Alessia was being asked to do the same—and so was he. Three marriages to save a monarchy.

'However, before I commit myself to a loveless marriage, I have conditions that must be agreed in writing.'

There was a long beat of silence before the queen asked, 'And those conditions are?'

'That Alessia and I do not live in the castle but in a suitable dwelling elsewhere on the estate. I will not have my life dictated by protocol within my own home. I will not have my life dictated by any means. So there are no ambiguities between us or things that can be left open to interpretation, let me be clear—I will not be a working member of your family. I will not attend palace functions that have the press corps in attendance, and that includes family functions like Prince Amadeo's wedding. I will not undertake royal engagements. I will never do anything intentionally that will cause harm to your family but I will live out of the spotlight and remain autonomous in how I conduct my life.' Ignoring the latest collective intake of breath, he continued with his demands. 'My word as my child's father will be absolute. Alessia and I will raise him how we see fit and there will be no argument or interference from any of you.'

At this, Alessia's eyes finally met his. He caught the surprise in them and…was that admiration? Whatever it was, one blink and it was gone, replaced by an indifference that bordered on contempt.

'Anything else?' Amadeo asked through gritted teeth.

'Yes. If we marry, it will be a private affair, and by private I mean immediate family only. No guests, no photographers, no press, just a simple statement after the deed has been done in which you can clarify my intention to live as a private person, and which brings me to my final condition—I will only marry Alessia if I have her personal assurance that she is in agreement and, as such, I ask you all to leave the room so we can discuss the matter in private.' He deliberately held Amadeo's stare. 'I need to be satisfied that she gives her consent freely, so if you will excuse us…'

He let his words hang in the air. He doubted any member of this family had ever been spoken to in such a manner before. He wasn't being deliberately provocative or disrespectful but he knew perfectly well that he needed to set his stall out early so there could be no misunderstandings.

The queen was the first to react. Rising to her feet—she was so short that even standing while the rest remained seated she barely reached her husband's and sons' heads—she looked him in the eye. 'Speak to my daughter privately, by all means, but as you have spoken so freely, allow me the same courtesy. Whatever you think, I love my daughter. Whether you marry her or not, I will support her. We all will. And we will weather any storm that comes our way in the same way we always do—as a family.'

With only the briefest inclination of her head, she summoned the men of her family to their feet. In silence, they followed her out, the two princes towering over their mother and throwing daggers of loathing at Gabriel, and were quickly followed by the lawyers and other assorted staff.

And then it was just him and Alessia.

Huge, painful thumps in his chest made it suddenly hard to breathe but he fought through it to try and read the beautiful face of the woman he'd shared the best night of his life with.

Gabriel was excellent at reading body language. While they'd waited in tense silence for Alessia to arrive, he'd read the body language of all the Berrutis. Both princes were mountains of barely concealed rage. He sensed Amadeo's fury was at the situation as a whole. Marcelo's, he suspected, was directed entirely at him, Gabriel. The queen was steely concerned only with damage limitation. The king's body language told him that he would, once again, be the family peacemaker. It was a role Gabriel understood all too well—it was the role within his own family that had propelled him into a making a career out of peace negotiations. The reasons for needing those peace negotiations were the same reasons he kept such tight control of his emotions and had always selected his lovers from a pool of reserved, emotionally austere women. That he was on the cusp of marrying a woman who had passion embedded in her DNA and who guaranteed the press intrusion he so despised were things he must learn to handle, and quickly.

Alessia was the only Berruti who'd kept her feelings in check during their talk. Other than that flicker of surprise when he'd informed the family in no uncertain terms that they would raise their child as *they* saw fit, she'd revealed nothing of her inner feelings. Even now, when it was just the two of them at opposing ends of the large, teak table, she simply sat in her chair, back straight, hands folded neatly on the table, eyes on him, giving nothing away other than haughty disdain.

He knew though, that her haughty façade was just that—a façade.

Born princess she might be, but it wasn't possible that the woman who'd sobbed in his arms and then come undone in them, who'd exploded with a passion so strong it had to be a fundamental part of her nature, could be as cold on the inside as she was showing on the outside. And he shouldn't be wishing her to reveal it.

Alessia willed herself to hold Gabriel's hard stare. The vast space between them had shrunk to nothing and it was a struggle to think over the blood rushing through her head to console herself that he was too far away to see the thuds of her heart beating so hard and fast through her chest.

She willed even harder for the tears to stay away.

She would not let the hurt he'd put her through leech out. He would never know how his early-morning disappearing act had devastated her.

'I have to say, this feels a rather extreme method of forcing you to see me again,' she said with airy nonchalance when the silence finally became too much, and was gratified to see his jaw clench. Allowing herself a tight smile, she got down to business. 'I am grateful that you have agreed to marry me and save my family from further scandal, and grateful for your concern about whether I consent freely to us marrying. As I'm sure you remember from the night we conceived our child, when we spoke of Amadeo's marriage, consent and free will are important to me. You have my assurance that I do consent.'

One of the thick black eyebrows that had so fascinated her that night rose. 'You consent to a loveless marriage?'

'Of course.' She smiled and added with a touch of sarcastic bite, 'After all, I'm from a family that puts duty before personal feelings. In that respect, I think it can only be a good thing to marry a man who will put our child's emotional needs first because I, like the rest of my family, am far too repressed to know how to do that. What a great example you'll be able to set to him or her.' Her smile widened. 'A *great* example. One day in the future, I must remember to tell them of the time when Daddy sneaked out of the castle after spending the night having sex with Mummy and then cold-shouldered her until he came riding in to rescue the conceived child from the horrors of a family without any mercy in them.' She mock shuddered before bestowing him with another, even brighter smile. 'Let me know when it's your birthday—I'll buy you a superhero cape with *SV* for Super Virtuous emblazoned on it.'

Fearing her charade was on the verge of cracking, Alessia rose and strode to the door, opened it and invited her anxious, waiting family back inside before Gabriel could find a response.

Alessia entered 'the zone,' a place she inhabited during certain interminably boring royal engagements. Being in the zone enabled her to put her happy face on and speak brightly and clearly while a pre-marriage contract was drawn up, read through, redrafted, read through again, more clauses removed, others added... And so it went on, and on, and on, the monotony broken by a regular supply of refreshment that she made sure to consume even though her stomach was so tightly cramped she had to force the food down her throat and into it.

Occasionally a stunned voice played in her ear: *You're planning a marriage to Gabriel Serres*, but she ignored it. Everything was too fantastical and happening too fast for it to actually feel real.

She was going to have to live with him and she couldn't even begin to dissect the swell of emotions that rose in her to think of what this would mean.

Time passed in a strange alchemy of speed and slowness. Though Alessia kept strictly to her side of the table, her awareness of Gabriel's presence within these four walls was as acute as if he were standing right beside her. He was too far from her to be able to smell him but she kept catching whiffs of cologne that made her abdomen clench and her pulses soar. She fought not to gaze at him. She also fought to not march over and slap his face, which frightened her as much as the yearning to stare.

Only when Gabriel was satisfied that it protected him from actually having to be a royal did he sign the contract, and then it was her turn. She wanted to fix him with another icy stare, prove her indifferent disdain, but by then her emotions were so heightened that it was all she could do to hold the pen. She added her signature to the document without the flourish she'd so wanted to make it with. Their respective lawyers acted as witnesses and made their marks too, and then it was done.

Her composure in severe danger of unravelling, Alessia left immediately, using the excuse that she wished to rest before dinner. Leaving before anyone else, she hurried out of the room avoiding Gabriel's attempt to catch her eye.

Her nausea had returned with a vengeance and she hurried along the wide corridors to her private quarters. She climbed the stairs, closed her bedroom door and ran into the bathroom, where she threw up straight into the toilet.

It seemed to take for ever before her stomach felt

settled enough for her to crawl off the floor and brush her teeth, and then she staggered back into the bedroom and collapsed on her bed.

Closing her eyes, she pressed a hand to her belly and breathed deeply, in and out. Having inherited her mother's petite figure and danced for exercise and enjoyment most days of her life, her stomach had always been flat. Early though the pregnancy was, there was a noticeable swelling, just as her breasts had swollen. As dream-like as everything had felt these last few days, one thing had made itself felt with concrete certainty. She was pregnant. Her body was doing what it needed to do to bring her baby safely into this world. And Alessia would do what was needed too, and that meant marrying Gabriel.

She'd expected coming face to face with him to be hard but she hadn't expected it to be that hard. She hadn't expected to feel so *much*.

Being a good, dutiful princess…that was Alessia's role in this world, her purpose, her reason for being.

Her comments about Dominic had been one unguarded moment but her night with Gabriel was a different matter entirely. That night, she had broken free from the bonds of duty and freed the real woman inside, and it was terrifying how strongly seeing Gabriel again relit that passionate fire inside her.

She was a *princess*.

There was a rap on her door.

Wishing the world would leave her alone, she sighed and closed her eyes tightly before calling out. 'I'm resting. Please come back in thirty minutes.'

The door opened.

Surprised, she lifted her head, but any mild rebuke to whoever had taken it on themselves to disturb her solitude fell from her lips when Gabriel marched into her bedroom.

CHAPTER FIVE

GABRIEL NOTED THE shock at his intrusion on Alessia's flushed face as she scrambled to sit up, gripping one of the four-poster bed's posts and pressing herself into it. He'd taken her by surprise in the one room in the whole castle she could expect privacy.

Too bad, he thought grimly. They were going to be married soon. Two strangers who'd spent one perfect night together were going to be tied together for life.

'Who let you in?' she whispered, pressing her cheek to the post. 'What do you want?'

'Your staff let me in—they know that they will soon be my staff too. As for what I want...?'

Did it matter what he wanted? No, was the concise answer. He'd envisaged his child's entire future in half a minute and known at the end of that flash into the future that his or her best chance of growing into a functional adult was with Gabriel a permanent, constant part of their life. That his own life would be uprooted and upended was irrelevant. He'd failed to use protection. His child had not chosen to be conceived. Therefore his wants were unimportant.

One want that was important, though, was a want for a cordial relationship with Alessia. He had no wish for a wife who despised him. He knew first-hand from his own parents' toxic hatred of each other the damage warring parents could do to a child.

He headed to a pale blue velvet armchair placed close to the bed. It was an elaborate piece of furniture that fitted in perfectly with the feminine vibes of the princess-perfect room. His sister, he thought, would have gladly killed for a bedroom like this. Although long used to riches, he had a feeling this castle would still blow Mariella's mind.

He could take only a small crumb of solace that Alessia's room, as with the brief impression he'd obtained of the rest of her quarters, had a warmer feel to it than her parents' quarters.

'I want to talk before I leave Ceres to sort my affairs,' he said.

'Why?'

He sat down and gazed at her steadily, trying his best to block the feminine scents of this most feminine of rooms much as he was trying to block the surging of his pulses. 'Why do you think? We've pledged to spend our lives together with only cursory words exchanged between us.'

'What else is there to say?' Bitterness seeped into her husky voice. 'We've agreed to marry and raise our child together. End of story.'

'Our story is only beginning. I had hoped to discuss things properly with you when we had that time alone together earlier but you used it to take cheap shots at me and then invited your family straight back in before I could give a rebuttal.'

The burn of her angry eyes blazed enough to penetrate his skin.

Gabriel took a deep breath. He'd made his point. Time to move on to what he'd sought her out for in the first place—to diffuse tensions. 'I never meant to imply that you and your family are incapable of loving a child.'

She released her hold on the bed post and straightened, her chin jutting. Her shock at his appearance was rapidly diminishing, the regal princess remerging from the vulnerable woman who'd scrambled with shock at his appearance in her room. With a glimmer of her earlier haughty disdain, she said, 'You didn't imply it. You were explicit about it.'

'If I offended you, I apologise.' He'd spoken the truth to make his point to Alessia and her family but, he conceded, it was a point he would have softened if he hadn't reacted so strongly to seeing her again. Those same feelings were rampaging through him now but he'd prepared for it before entering her room and that mental preparation made it possible for him to choose his words with his usual care. He could look at the rosebud lips and sultry dark velvet eyes, and temper the awareness coursing through him so that it became nothing but a distant thrum.

'Apology accepted,' she said curtly, wriggling elegantly to press her back against the velvet headboard. 'Now please leave. I'm tired and wish to rest.'

'Not yet.' He rested his elbows on his thighs. 'We marry in three days and—'

The composure Alessia had only just found shattered. 'What are you talking about? I thought the wedding would be in a few weeks?'

'If you hadn't run away from the meeting, you would know this.'

'I didn't run away—I thought everything had been agreed.'

'Only the basics. Everything else is to be decided between you and me, which is why I am here.'

'Everything like what?'

'Our marriage. How we're going to make it work so that we can live together and raise a child together.'

Icy panic clutched her chest. Three days was nothing. How was she supposed to prepare herself in that time? It was impossible. Three days! Three days until she became the wife of the man who'd ghosted her? It was too soon! She'd thought she had weeks! 'Who decided we'd marry in three days?' she demanded to know, unable to keep the agitation from her voice.

'It was a collective decision. Your family worry that news of our marriage will take the spotlight from Amadeo's wedding. We marry on Thursday and release the news on Friday. The press then have over a month to milk it until it curdles before Amadeo's wedding takes place.'

'And you agreed to this?'

He shrugged. 'Your family agreed to all my conditions. It was only fair I give them a concession in return.'

'How magnanimous of you,' she spat, hating that his composure was as assured as ever while all her turmoil was showing itself, feelings heightened by him sitting close enough to her that it wasn't the ghost of his cologne seeping into her senses as it had been during the meeting but his actual cologne, splashed on his cheeks and neck after he'd shaved that morning. It made her remember how she'd buried her face in his neck and inhaled his scent so greedily, which only made the feelings heighten. She didn't want to feel anything for this man or to show anything but the deserved contempt she'd managed earlier, but everything she'd had drilled in her the entirety of her life had slipped out of reach. They could be talking about the weather for all the emotion Gabriel was showing and she hated him for it. 'How truly *benevolent.*'

Gabriel recognised that Alessia's cool façade from earlier had been well and truly stripped away. He'd been right—it *had* all been a façade. Beneath the haughty exterior, she'd seethed with emotion. For whose benefit had she chosen to hide it? His or her family's?

He stared deep into those blazing velvet eyes again, the thrum of awareness heightening. She wanted an argument, he realised. Gabriel did not fight, physically or verbally, and never would. His parents' marriage had been too volatile even in the supposedly happy years for him to ever allow himself to follow in their shoes and lose his calm, and it was unnerving to find himself responding to the passionate emotions Alessia was brimming with.

With a sickening jolt, he realised it was this passion that had sang to him that night.

Making love with Alessia was the only time in his adult life he'd lost control of himself, and the thrumming of awareness thickened to fully realise for the first time that marriage meant he no longer had to bury his desire for her.

Closing his eyes briefly, he inhaled to control the tightening in his loins. To regain control of his thoughts. To regain control of the biting emotions.

He shifted his chair forwards and locked back onto Alessia's fiery stare. Making sure to pitch his voice at its usual modulated tone, he said, 'Considering that marrying you means I have to give up the career I excel at and move to a new country, I would say my conditions were reasonable and justified.'

'No one asked you to give up your job.'

'Once news of our marriage hits the press it will be impossible for me to continue. My clients employ me because I guarantee results and my discretion is guaranteed. Once I become a public figure, the anonymity I rely on to do my job effectively is gone.'

She pulled her knees to her chest and rested her chin on them in the same way she'd done when he'd first found himself falling under her spell. 'I'm sure you'll find a way to adapt it to the new circumstances.'

'Adaptation is always possible, of course, but continuing the business as it is will not.'

'You don't have to marry me. No one's putting a gun to your head.'

'I've put a metaphorical gun to my own head. Secrets don't stay secret. Even if we didn't marry, as soon as the pregnancy starts to show speculation about the father will start and sooner or later my name will leak, and I'll still be thrust into the spotlight I never wanted. Either way, my life as it is is over, which leaves me only two choices—marry you and be a permanent feature in my child's life, or don't and leave everything about my child's upbringing to chance. If there is one thing you will learn about me it is that I do not leave anything to chance.'

'And you don't think I'll be a loving mother,' she stated, tremulously. The implication had wounded her. Alessia had only known she was pregnant a few days but, once the tears had dried, her heart had swollen with an emotion she struggled to define, a combination of excitement and fear and love. Love for a fledging being that probably didn't as yet have a heartbeat.

Many times over the years she'd wondered what kind of mother she would be. The only conclusion she'd reached was that she'd be a different mother to her own, but she couldn't say that to Gabriel. It wasn't just a matter of disloyalty but because he wouldn't understand. How could he? A monarch wasn't an ordinary person and, even with the best will in the world, they couldn't be an ordinary parent. Their number one priority had to be to the monarchy. Alessia, though, would never be a monarch, and she thanked the good Lord every day for that.

Gabriel's eyes had narrowed but when he answered, his words were measured. 'I think you're capable of it but you're from a world where duty comes first and often to the detriment of the individual. Look at you and your brothers—all of you marrying for one reason or other to save the monarchy. I will not have our child feel forced to make those same choices.'

'It's a choice *you're* making too.'

'For their sake,' he replied in the same measured tone. 'And it is up to you and me to make the best of it and create a stable home for them. It will take many compromises and concessions on both our parts but if we are both willing, then it is achievable.'

'Will you compromise on coming to Amadeo's wedding with me?' she retorted, already knowing how humiliating it would be to attend Ceres's biggest state event in decades without her new husband by her side. People would understand someone wanting to remain private and not wanting to be a working royal, but family events, even when they were state occasions, were different. Gabriel's refusal to attend could only be interpreted as personal.

'My conditions have already been agreed but everything else is open to negotiation. The question is, are *you* willing to make the compromises and concessions necessary for our child?'

How could this be the same man who'd made love to her with such frenzied passion? Alessia wondered, gazing at him in disbelief. From the expression on Gabriel's face and the tone of his voice, he could be conducting an ordinary business meeting, not discussing the upturning of both their worlds; and his world was being upturned far more than her own.

On paper, he was everything she'd ever wanted in a husband. He was everything she'd waited for—a man she could respect, who made her feel and who wouldn't sell her out. Gabriel commanded respect just by walking in a room, and there was no denying he made her feel. In the short hours they'd spent together, he'd made her feel more intensely than she'd ever felt in her life, more than she'd believed it was possible to feel. Even now, after he'd cold-shouldered her for two weeks, the intensity of her awareness for him hadn't diminished at all. Watching his mouth as he spoke, taking in the stubble thickening on his jaw, catching those whiffs of his cologne…it all did something to her. Meeting his eye was even worse, and now she was stuck on her bed with her veins buzzing, her heart a pulsating mess, hugging her legs as tightly as she could so he couldn't see the tremors wracking her. So yes, as much as she wished he didn't, it was undeniable that he made her feel.

She knew too that he would never sell her out. His clients' loss was her gain; Gabriel's discretion was assured. And he'd made it clear he took fatherhood seriously. She should be rejoicing that he ticked all the husband boxes.

But he felt nothing for her. He wouldn't be her prince. He'd left her sleeping and disappeared from her life as if what they'd shared had never been… But it had been. The tiny life in her belly was proof of that.

She breathed in deeply and kneaded the back of her neck. It scared her how badly she wanted the man who'd created that life with her, who'd made love to her with such intense passion, who'd brought the woman out in her, to resurface.

'Alessia?' he said, one of his thick black eyebrows raising at her silence.

She blinked her thoughts away and took a deep breath before meeting his gaze. 'Yes,' she said. 'I am willing to make compromises and concessions for the sake of our child.'

'That is good to hear. It will make life easier for all concerned if we always strive for common ground.'

Unable to speak about her marriage—an event she'd always looked forward to with rose-coloured lenses—any further in such an emotionless way, Alessia changed the subject. 'Was anything else agreed while my back was turned?'

'Yes. The converted stable block is going to be our home here. Your father tells me it is in need of modernising. Once we have agreed what we want from the renovations, the work on it will begin immediately.'

The stable block in question sat apart from the two main turreted mishmash of buildings that constituted the castle, and had initially been converted for Alessia's widowed grandmother to live in when her daughter took the throne on her husband's death. The dowager queen had been a cantankerous old boot who'd loathed living in the castle surrounded by the thing she hated most: people. And so the stable block had been converted into a seven-bedroom dwelling which she'd taken great delight in not admitting anyone into. Alessia had been terrified of her but also secretly fascinated. It had been this grandmother whose haughty spirit she'd channelled earlier to get her through seeing Gabriel again without falling to pieces. She'd tried hard to reach for that spirit again since he'd barged his way into her room but she couldn't find it any more. Knowing her grandmother, she'd probably hidden from her out of spite from her perch in heaven.

Knowing her grandmother, she would have adored Gabriel. A man who seemingly disdained the monarchy as much as she had marrying into the family would have thrilled her. The difference was that her grandmother had been from the old Greek royal family and had played her public part as queen consort until her husband's death magnificently. For all his talk about compromise, Gabriel had been very clear that when it came to royal life, he would have nothing to do with it and that there would be no compromise on this, not even for Amadeo's wedding. Alessia would be a princess with a husband but without a prince for the rest of her life.

Fearing the swelling of emotions filling back up in her, Alessia straightened her legs and spine, and lifted her chin. 'Anything else?'

'That's everything that was discussed.'

'Good. Then I would be grateful if you would leave. I'm tired and wish to rest before dinner.'

He eyed her meditatively. 'Before I go, I would like to apologise.'

'You've already apologised.'

'This is a different matter. I wish to apologise for not returning your call.'

It felt like he'd plunged an icy hand into her heart. The impulse to draw her knees back to her chest was strong, but she fought it. 'Oh. That,' she said with an airiness she had no idea how she achieved. 'Don't worry about it—it was a mere whim. I just thought if you ever came back to Ceres and was at a loose end then we could go out for drinks. I'd forgotten I even made the call.'

'Whatever your reasons for calling, it was unforgivably rude of me to not return it. I will not insult your intelligence by making up excuses. A great part of me did want to call you back but the reason I didn't is because I knew that nothing could happen between us. You're a princess and I'm a man who values my privacy and anonymity. The two are not compatible.'

How she managed to meet his stare after those words, she would never know. But she did. She forced herself to, and she forced herself to hold it. What she couldn't do was stop the tremor that came into her voice. 'Then you will have to agree it's ironic that you're being forced to marry a woman you're not compatible with.'

There was a long moment of stillness before Gabriel got to his feet. Slowly, he stepped to the bed and leaned his face down to hers.

His eyes were ringing with that beautiful supernova of golden colour she'd seen the night they'd made love and, though she tried hard to fight it, a tingle of electricity raced up her spine and tightened her skin.

His firm lips tugged into something that nearly resembled a smile but there was nothing ambiguous about the pulsating of his eyes. 'No one is forcing me to marry you, Alessia.' His face was so close to hers his hot breath caressed her face just as his tone caressed the rest of her senses. 'Our lives are not compatible and it is unlikely we have compatibility in our interests… But there is one area where we *know* we are compatible.'

The flush that crawled through her was the deepest and hottest she had ever known. She felt it crawl through every cell in her body, burning her from the inside out, and when his face moved even closer, she could no longer draw breath.

'We can have a successful marriage,' he whispered, the tips of their noses touching. 'And we can have a fulfilling one too.'

Her lips were buzzing manically even before Gabriel's mouth brushed lightly to them, but still that first touch landed like a thrill that filled her mouth with moisture and made her pelvis contract into a tight pulse.

She hadn't even realised she'd closed her eyes until the delicious pressure against her lips vanished and she opened them to find Gabriel upright and gazing down at her with that sensual, hooded expression she remembered so well.

She couldn't open her throat to speak.

His shoulders rose as he breathed in deeply, then,

wordlessly, he reached into his back pocket and pulled out his wallet. From it, he plucked a business card. Eyes still boring intently into hers, he handed it to her.

She still couldn't open her throat to speak, could barely raise an eyebrow in question.

'My personal number,' he said with the hint of wry smile. 'Call me at any time. If I don't answer, I will call you back. I give you my word.'

At the door he gave one last inclination of his head. 'Until our wedding day.'

Gabriel took a moment to compose himself before going back downstairs.

The thrills racing through his loins stretched the moment to an age.

Only when certain his arousal was contained did he take the steps down.

As he left the castle, acknowledging a dozen members of staff along the way, he acknowledged too the satisfaction of a job well done.

The sexiest woman in the world was carrying his child and he'd successfully negotiated a marriage to her in which he would not be tainted by the celebrity of monarchy or controlled by her family, and in which he could continue living his life as a private man. Undeniably, he had to wind down the business that had been the biggest part of his life for such a long time, but at the end of negotiations, it was the gains you made that counted, not the losses, and his gains were ones he could live with.

He was certain too that soon Alessia would appreciate the gains *she'd* made in the negotiations. A husband and protector for their child.

And a lover for herself.

Two a.m. and Alessia was still wide awake. There was so much going through her head, so much to process, that sleep was impossible.

What a day. What a month. Part of her wished desperately that she could wind back time to Marcelo and Clara's wedding reception and gag her own mouth. But that was only a small part of her because wishing to reverse time meant wishing the life in her belly out of existence and she could never wish for that. That fledgling life was already a part of her and a growing part of her heart had already attached itself to it.

Switching her bedside light on, she reached for the business card she'd laid by her book. Her heart in her mouth, she lightly traced a finger over the numbers printed on it.

Impulse, much like the ones that had made her call out to him and swing herself over the balustrade into his balcony, had her grab her phone and dial the number.

It was answered on the third ring.

'Alessia?' His voice was thick with sleep.

Blinking with surprise that he'd guessed it was her, all she could say was, 'Yes.'

'Are you okay?'

She closed her eyes as the deep, smooth timbre poured into her ear and sent tingles racing through her, and gave a long, soft inhale. 'Gabriel…?'

'Yes?' he said quietly into the silence.

She drew her knees to her chest and took a deeper breath. 'You do know it's a huge risk that you're taking?'

'What is?'

'Marrying me. The pregnancy is at such an early stage…the most dangerous stage.' Her voice dropped even lower. 'My mother had three miscarriages between me and Marcelo. It's why there's such a big age gap between us. I'll do everything I can to bring our child safely into the world but sometimes nature has other ideas. Are you prepared for that? That our marriage might be for nothing?'

This time the silence came from him. When he answered, his voice was the gentlest she'd ever heard it. 'I am marrying you for our child's sake, Alessia, but it is you I am committing myself to. Whatever the future holds for us, it is a commitment I am making for the rest of my life.'

Tears filled her eyes, and she had to squeeze them tightly to stop them falling. 'I'm sorry for waking you.'

'Don't be.'

Her voice was barely a whisper as she wished him a goodnight.

CHAPTER SIX

ALESSIA'S WEDDING DAY arrived in a blaze of glorious sunshine. Wearing only skimpy silk pyjamas, she stepped onto her balcony and welcomed the rays sinking into skin that had felt so cold when she'd pulled herself out of the earlier nightmare.

'Good morning, Alessia.'

Startled, she whipped her head to the adjoining balcony. Gabriel emerged to stand at the balustrade, coffee in hand. Her stomach flipped, her heart setting off at a canter at the sight of him. All he wore was a pair of low-slung black shorts that perfectly showed off his taut abdomen and snake hips, his bronzed, muscular chest bare and gleaming under the sun, hair mussed and the stubble on his face grown so thick it should rightly be called a beard.

'What are you doing here?' she asked dumbly, unable to scramble the wits together to stop herself from staring. She swore he grew more devastatingly handsome each time she saw him.

A faint curve of a smile. 'I flew in last night.'

'No one told me.'

He raised a hefty shoulder and took a sip of his coffee. 'I dislike being late. My immediate affairs were all in order so I thought it prudent to arrive early. It meant there were less things that could go wrong today. You'd already retired for the night when the decision was made.' His eyes narrowed, deep lines forming in his brow. 'You look tired. Are you still not sleeping?'

With the memory of that awful dream, which had come after it had taken her hours to fall back to sleep after the previous one, still fresh in her mind, she shook her head. 'Bad dreams.'

She'd been chasing her mother through the castle screaming for her, but her mother had been deaf to her cries. Then she'd found herself in the old, disused banqueting hall. Gabriel and Amadeo had been in there, dining together, but they'd been deaf and blind to her too.

She'd had much worse dreams before but this was the only one she'd woken from sobbing.

There was a brief flare of concern. 'Anything you wish to share?'

'It's bad luck to share a dream before midday unless you want it to come true.'

'You don't believe that superstitious nonsense, do you?'

'No. But just in case, I'm not going to risk it by telling you.'

His firm lips curved into the first real smile he'd bestowed on her. It transformed his face into something that made her already weak legs go all watery and a deep throb pulse inside her, somehow managing to make him look a decade younger despite the crinkles around his eyes and the grooves that appeared down the sides of his mouth.

Her returning smile didn't falter when a glamorous woman of around thirty dressed in a kimono-style robe and with her dark hair piled messily but artfully on top of her head appeared on his balcony and padded like a panther to stand beside him.

'Buenos días,' the woman said, rising on her toes to plant a kiss on Gabriel's cheek.

The violence of the nausea that caught hold of Alessia at this was so strong she pressed both hands to her abdomen. So loud was the roaring in her head that she almost missed Gabriel's introduction.

'Alessia, this is my sister, Mariella.'

His sister?

There hadn't been time for her to think about who this woman could be, but the spinning sensation that had her clutching the balustrade was undoubtedly relief, and she only realised Gabriel had introduced her in Spanish when Mariella's eyes widened and she dropped into a deep curtsey.

'You don't have to do that,' Alessia croaked. 'Please, Gabriel,' she added when his sister lifted her head and looked at her non-comprehendingly, and her own proficiency in Spanish had deserted her, 'tell her not to do that.'

Not taking his eyes off Alessia's flushed face, Gabriel translated while his mind whirled with what could have caused the strange turn she'd just had.

Pregnancy hormones? Whatever the cause, the same needle of concern that had fired in his blood when she'd called him in the middle of the night pierced him again.

She'd sounded so vulnerable that night. He'd laid awake a long time after that call wondering whether he should fly back to Ceres. It still disturbed him how strong the pull had been.

It disturbed him too how hard a thump his heart had made when he'd recognised the number flashing on his phone and how deep the prickles that had covered his skin when her voice first seeped into his ear.

Having no need to fight himself from thinking about her any more, Alessia had unleashed in his mind a permanent vision that must have blurred because, looking at her now, she was more impossibly beautiful than his mind's eye had remembered. As his thoughts now skipped forwards to their wedding night, anticipation let loose in his blood and he came to the realisation that there was nothing disturbing in his reactions to her. Quite the opposite. He should be celebrating that he was pledging his life to a woman who aroused him more than any woman before her.

Yes, he thought thickly. Much better that he felt the pull to be with her than the alternative.

Mariella pushed herself up off the floor, and pulled Gabriel's thoughts away from the sensual delights the evening promised.

'Please,' Alessia said in that same strange croaky voice, placing a hand on the balustrade next to his, 'tell her we don't stand on ceremony.'

Unable to resist, he covered it with his own and was gratified when, though her eyes widened and more colour saturated her cheeks, she made no effort to move it. Pressing his abdomen against the cold stone, he leaned his face closer to hers and dropped his voice. 'You wish for me to lie to her?'

'But we don't,' she protested, her indignation making her sound a fraction more like her usual self.

'Perhaps not compared to your ancestors,' he agreed lightly. The compulsion to reach over the balustrade, grip her handspan waist and lift her over it and to him sent a throb rippling through his loins. She was so tiny, well over a foot shorter than him and roughly half his weight, and yet they had fit together so well. *Perfectly* well, he recalled with another throb in his loins. Like two pieces of a two-piece jigsaw...

'We don't,' she insisted, bringing *her* face closer to *his* with a piqued glare. 'Please tell your sister that I'm delighted to meet her and that I look forward to getting to know her.'

An unexpected zip of humour tugged at him at her formal tone but, remembering they had an audience, he reluctantly moved his hand, took a step back and made the translation.

The Berrutis did not expect commoners to bow and scrape to them any more, he conceded, but there was an absolute expectation of deference. From the expression on Alessia's face, this expectation was so deeply ingrained that she likely didn't realise it was there. In fairness to her, there was nothing he'd seen of her behaviour to indicate she thought herself better than anyone else. She didn't parade on her royal dignity like so many royal people were wont to do, Amadeo, her eldest brother, being one of them. But she was oblivious to how elegant and regal her bearing was, even when dishevelled, wearing pyjama shorts that perfectly displayed her toned, golden legs and a strappy pyjama top her small breasts jutted against. Her perfect breasts, he remembered thickly as he slowly swept his gaze over her again. They'd tasted so sweet. Fitted in the palms of his hands. And as he feasted his eyes on her, another flush of colour crept over her face, and the tips of those perfect breasts became visible through the silk of her pyjama top.

She was extraordinary. As desirable a creature as he had ever seen. Her dark, velvet eyes were locked on his, an expression in them he recognised: it had lodged itself in his retinas in that breath of a moment before their lips had first fused together. Unfiltered want. Want for him.

Mariella tugged at his arm, pulling him out of the strange, heady trance-for-two he'd become frozen in. Dragging his gaze from Alessia's, he stooped down a little so his sister could whisper in his ear.

He cleared his throat and translated for Alessia. 'Mariella says it's bad luck for us to see each other before the wedding.'

She blinked before responding. Then blinked again. The heightened colour still stained her cheeks but she pulled—and he swore he saw the effort it took to achieve it—a smile to her face. Taking a step back, she said lightly, 'You don't believe in that superstitious nonsense, do you?'

'I don't believe in superstition.'

'Neither to do I, but as with my dream, I don't want to take risks so I'm going to use your sister's reminder as an excuse to go back inside. I'll see you at the chapel.' Then she turned to Mariella and, in almost perfect Spanish, said, 'It was a pleasure to meet you,' before she padded into the quarters he'd be sharing with her before the night was out.

Alessia reached for the glass of water on her dressing table and tried to quench her parched mouth, but her hand trembled so hard more water ended up spilling down her chin than down her throat. A drop splashed on her wedding dress. It felt like a portent.

She'd chosen a simple white silk dress with spaghetti straps that formed a V at the cleavage and a short train that splayed behind her. The royal beauty team had worked their magic, pulling her hair into a loose knot with white flowers carefully entwined into it and loose tendrils framing her face. Subtle makeup and a subtly elegant diamond tiara placed on top of the sheer veil completed the look. The simplicity of the dress had felt fitting for the simplicity of the wedding when she'd chosen it, but looking at it now, all she felt was an unbearable sadness. The dress, like everything, was the opposite of what she'd envisaged whenever she'd daydreamed about her perfect wedding day.

Her father entered the room. Placing his hands on

her arms, he kissed her temple, then stepped back to take a proper look at her. 'You look beautiful.'

She tried to smile but couldn't make her mouth work.

He looked at her awhile longer then sighed and said heavily, 'You don't have to do this.'

She met his eyes. 'I do.'

'No.' He sighed again. 'It feels wrong. No one will blame you if you change your mind.'

She thought again of the barely suppressed fury in her mother's eyes when the family had confronted her about the pregnancy. It was a look she'd never seen from her before, worse than the reproach from her unguarded comments about Dominic, and she prayed she'd never see it again. The angry censure had been in all her blood family's eyes. But not Marcelo, she remembered wistfully. His eyes had been full of sympathy. He'd known exactly how she was feeling because he'd been there himself, trying to fix a mess of his own making.

Their family, though, had never looked at him with the same disappointment they'd looked at Alessia. Their reproval had been laced with understanding of his nature. Their forgiveness for him had come easily.

'*I'll* blame me,' she told her father, whose troubled eyes told her he, at least, had forgiven her. 'I wouldn't be able to live with myself if my actions led to the destruction of the monarchy.' The smile she'd tried to conjure finally came, small though it was, and she took her father's hand and gave it a reassuring squeeze. 'This is for the best. We can trust Gabriel with our family. If we honour our side of the deal, he'll honour his.' Of that, she was certain.

It was the only certainty she had about him.

Shortly, she would leave her quarters and marry a man she knew so little of that when a woman had appeared on his balcony on her wedding morning, Alessia's automatic assumption was that the woman had been his lover.

She knew so little about him that she didn't know if he did have a lover tucked away somewhere. She didn't know if Mariella was his only sibling.

But there was one more thing she did know, and it frightened her badly. That brief moment earlier on the balcony when she'd automatically assumed Mariella to be his lover…it had felt like she'd been hit by a truck. The relief to learn she was his sister had been dizzying, and then she'd found herself trapped in Gabriel's stare…

She'd seen the desire in his eyes. She'd seen it and been helpless to stop herself from reacting to it, no more than she'd been unable to stop the swelling of her heart when he'd smiled and his face had lit up into something heartbreaking.

So that's the one more thing she knew—how he made her feel. Like a giddy, jealous schoolgirl. And it's what frightened her so badly too.

She didn't want to feel like that for him, full stop. She believed in the commitment he was about to make to her as his wife but she couldn't forget how he'd ignored her. If not for their baby, she would never have seen him again because he didn't think her worth the bother due to their supposed incompatibility. He'd never given her a chance to find out if they could be compatible in ways that didn't involve sex for the simple reason that he hadn't wanted to.

And she couldn't forget how devastated she'd been when she woke up to find him gone.

The Berrutis royal chapel was much bigger than Gabriel had envisaged and so ancient he could feel its history seeping through the high, stone walls and dome ceiling. He could feel his sister's awe at it all as she stood next to him while they waited for the bride to arrive. He could feel the Berruti family's bemusement at his choice of a woman for a best man and that the glamorous best man had donned a feminine tuxedo to match his own. Clara, the newest family member, had clapped her hands in glee at Mariella's outfit.

Gabriel had few friends. He could travel to almost any country in the world and find hospitality from friendly acquaintances, but true friends were rare. Partly this was because of his nomadic lifestyle, always basing himself wherever his current job was located. Partly it was because he liked his own company and would much rather spend a rare evening off sipping a large bourbon and watching a film noir or reading a good thriller. The only person he was close to was his sister. Two years younger than him, they'd been as close as siblings could be since before Mariella was out of nappies. Living in their family's war zone had cemented their closeness. Trusting her implicitly, he'd confided the entire Alessia and baby situation. There had been no judgement or efforts to tell him he was being a fool to throw his life away by marrying a stranger. She knew him well enough not to bother wasting her breath like that.

'Mum would wet herself if she could see this,' Mariella murmured. 'You, marrying a princess in a royal chapel.'

He gave a subtle mock shudder. 'I can well believe it.' Their mother was the most horrendous social climber, a born attention seeker and the root cause of his media hatred. The only thing that stopped her exposing Gabriel as her son to her countless social media followers was the hefty monthly allowance he paid her. A royal wedding, though, no matter how small, would be a temptation too far for her and so he'd made the decision not to invite her. This was his last event as a private person. The circus his life was going to turn into, one that made his guts twist to imagine, could wait a few days longer.

Movement broke the stillness of the chapel and jolted his heart. The bride had arrived. His bride.

Clutching her father's arm, she walked towards him. The closer she came, the clearer she became and the greater his heart swelled.

When she reached him, he carefully lifted the sheer veil. Her eyes locked with his. The swelling in his heart stopped and his chest tightened, crushing it. His jaw locked. Alessia was simply breathtaking. He'd never imagined such beauty existed.

For a long moment she stared at him, then her shoulders rose and she jutted her chin. 'Ready?'

He nodded.

'Good.' She smiled tightly. 'Then let's do this.'

Had there ever been a more miserable excuse for a wedding? Alessia wondered morosely. No wedding march. Only six guests and a priest. She signed her name to the certificate and thought of her large, extended family. They would have loved to be here. She would have loved for them to be here. The only moment that had matched her dreams had been the wedding kiss to seal their vows. Gabriel's eyes had pulsed with a heady sensuality and the promise of more before his warm lips had brushed hers, but even that had been tainted because she couldn't forget that she wasn't his choice for a bride. He wanted her, that was obvious, and he'd said as much in words and body language, but he'd never wanted to want her.

She wished she didn't want him. She wished the woman he'd unlocked in her would go back into hiding.

The ring he'd slid on her finger felt too weighty. She wished she could wrench it off.

Once Marcelo and Clara had signed their parts of the certificate as witnesses, they all left the chapel, cutting through the chapel garden to return to the castle, where a mockery of a banquet had been prepared for them.

'Where's the photographer?' Clara asked as they walked the winding footpath.

'There isn't one,' Gabriel informed her.

'Then can I take a picture of you both? For posterity?'

'That would be nice,' Alessia said at the exact same moment Gabriel politely said, 'The agreement was no photos, but thank you for the offer.'

It was seeing the disbelief on her sister-in-law's face that made Alessia crack and, suddenly frightened she was going to burst into tears, she sped off.

She would not cry in front of Gabriel again.

A hand caught her wrist.

'What's wrong?' Gabriel asked.

'Nothing,' she muttered, loosening her arm from him and setting off again. His legs being much longer than hers, he caught her in seconds and stood before her, blocking her path.

'Clearly something is wrong.' Not an auspicious start to married life, Gabriel thought wryly. 'If I have upset you, you must tell me, else how can I fix it?'

Velvet eyes snapped onto his. 'I don't understand why you don't want pictures taken.'

He strove for patience. 'It was one of my conditions for marrying you. If you had a problem with it you should have said when you had the chance.'

'You made it very clear they were take it or leave it conditions.' She twisted as if to barge past him but then stopped and folded her arms tightly around her chest and raised her chin to meet his stare again. 'You got your way about everything with this wedding.'

'Not the date,' he said lightly, trying to defuse the head of steam she was clearly building up.

'No, that came from my family. Not from me. In fact, not once did you or any of my family ask what *I* wanted from our wedding day.'

'And what did you want?'

'It's a bit late to ask me that now, isn't it?' she suddenly shouted, before kneading the back of her neck and making a visible effort to calm herself. 'I apologise. You were upfront about your conditions and the only thing that really bothered me about them at the time was your refusal to attend Amadeo's wedding and other family events the press will be at, but I didn't really think about our wedding in emotional terms until I put my dress on this morning. I chose this dress because it fitted the simple wedding we were having but my dream was always to wear an elaborate fairy-tale dress with a twelve-foot train and to have a dozen bridesmaids. I always envisaged my entire family and all my friends being there, and a truckload of confetti being tipped over my and the groom's heads, and a huge party afterwards that went on until the sun came up, but I didn't have any of that. So many people I love forbidden to be here, and now I'm not even allowed one photo as a reminder of my wedding day.'

Gabriel stared at the hurt on her face, the same hurt that had sounded in her husky voice, and wondered if she'd been given lessons on how to make a man feel like a heel. He had nothing to feel bad about, he knew that. He'd been upfront and open, unlike his bride, who'd clearly festered about the wedding day she believed her due and which she felt had been denied her. But she'd agreed to this. As she would say, he hadn't put a gun to her head. She'd agreed to this marriage of her own free will and agreed to his conditions, so it was a bit rich to start complaining once the deed was done.

Closing her eyes, she kneaded the back of her neck again and breathed deeply. Then her eyes fluttered open and fixed back on his. 'Ignore me. I'm just feeling a little more emotional than I expected and it's making me unreasonable.'

With an apologetic smile, she set off back down the path.

Gabriel watched her. The sun high above her seemed to cast her in a golden glow. For a moment he could believe she'd been conjured by an enchantment.

'You're not being unreasonable,' he called out, speaking through a boulder that had lodged in his throat.

She turned her head.

He breached the distance between them and gazed down at the pretty heart-shaped face and those sultry velvet eyes. A wave of desire sliced through him. Whether they could ever find common ground to build a successful marriage or not, she was now his wife, and she was breathtaking. There was not a man alive who wouldn't ache to share a bed with her.

Her chest rose, lifting those perfect, pert breasts. The desire tightened, making his skin tauten.

Colour rose on her cheeks. The tips of her breasts strained through the silk of her dress. He leaned his face closer. Her lips parted and her breath quickened. Whatever his wife's personal feelings about him, she wanted him. He could practically smell the desire radiating from her.

'And you're right,' he finally added. 'This is our wedding day. We should have photos to remember it by.' Then he placed his lips to a pretty, delicate ear and whispered thickly, 'And then, tonight, I will give you something else to remember this day by.'

The wedding banquet was as sorry an affair as the wedding itself but Alessia dragged it out as long as she could, eating at the same pace she'd done as a child when she'd wanted to annoy her brothers, who'd been forbidden from leaving the table until everyone had finished. She'd perfected the art of nibbling then and she brought those skills back out now. However, if Gabriel was annoyed at this, he hid it well, eating and drinking and conversing as if it were any meal for any occasion while she was filled with so many emotions that she didn't know how her knotted stomach was admitting food into it. All she could think was that once this banquet was done, the 'celebrations' would be over, and then she and Gabriel would go to her quarters. *Their* quarters.

As much as she tried to block them, his seductive words before he'd called Clara over to take photos of them kept ringing in her head. Every time she recalled them, heat flushed through her, a powerful throb deep in her pelvis sucking the air from her lungs. The same things happened every time she met his eye and caught the anticipatory gleam in them. Frightened at the strength of her desire for him, she tried hard not to look at him, but it was like Gabriel were a magnet her eyes were drawn to.

There were so many knots forming inside her that she couldn't work out if it was dread or excitement causing them. Or a mixture of both. Their night together had been so wonderful that the thought of experiencing it all again was almost too tantalising to bear, but the way Gabriel had left her the next morning and then ghosted her... Her new husband had hurt her badly, and if she didn't protect herself, she feared he would hurt her again.

She hated that her body and her head, the woman and the princess, were at such odds. Until she found a way to marry the two, she didn't know how she could dare risk letting him touch her and risk losing her head like she'd done the first time with him.

'Have you decided when you're going on honeymoon?' Clara asked from across the table.

Alessia had a drink of her water, wishing it was wine. 'We're not having one.'

Clara looked like she had something to say about this but Marcelo whispered in her ear and she clamped her lips together.

A honeymoon was something else Alessia would miss out on. And being carried across a threshold... She'd fantasised about that many times, being swept into her hunky husband's arms and carried through the door and laid lovingly on their marital bed...

She grabbed her spoon and stabbed it into her ricotta and cinnamon trifle, and gritted her teeth. She needed to stop these foolish thoughts. It was done. She'd married him.

As her old headmistress had loved to espouse,

she'd made her bed and now she had to lie in it. What her old headmistress had not espoused was how this was supposed to be achieved when one had to share that bed with a man it was imperative she protect her heart against.

CHAPTER SEVEN

THE BEATS OF Gabriel's heart were heavy as he followed Alessia into what was now their shared quarters, at least until the renovations of the converted stable block were completed. When he'd visited her after their marriage had been agreed, he hadn't taken much notice of any of it other than her bedroom but now he craned his neck around the high walls to take in the sumptuous furnishings, many of which he suspected were family heirlooms centuries old and much of which were too large for the rooms that were, surprisingly, the same size as the ones in the quarters he'd stayed in. They could never be described as small but in comparison to her parents' and brother's quarters, they were as pint-sized as the princess who lived in them. But there was plenty of modernity there too, the new blending perfectly with the old to create an eclectic apartment that was feminine and chic and regal all rolled into one. Although not to his taste, it was an apartment that suited Alessia perfectly and he couldn't deny the throb in his loins to know that soon—very soon—they would share that princess bed.

His new wife, who'd walked silently with her hands clasped together from the banquet room to their quarters, kicked her shoes off and hovered in the day room doorway, not looking at him. 'I need to shower so I'll leave you to familiarise yourself with the place. It's virtually the same as the quarters you stayed in so you shouldn't get lost.'

'Where has my stuff been put?' He'd been told his suitcases would be moved to his new quarters and his possessions unpacked for him.

She swallowed. 'In my dressing room. Come, I'll show you.'

He followed her up the stairs and caught the brief hesitation before she opened the bedroom door.

She padded across the room and opened the dressing room door. 'I've made as much room for you as I can but I'm afraid it's quite small—this section of the castle is four hundred years old, so relatively modern compared to other parts, and was once lodgings for courtiers until my great-grandparents had them all fiddled about with to create family apartments. This one and the one you stayed in are by far the smallest and were intended for visiting family but it was always my favourite, I don't know why, and when I came of age, I asked to have it rather than move into the one earmarked for me. The only thing missing from it was a dressing room so they stole space from the guest bedroom to create one for me.'

She paused for breath, a sheepish expression crossing her face. 'A very long-winded way of telling you that there isn't much space for your things. I'm sorry. I had all my ball gowns moved into the guest room, so if you find it all too cramped, you can put some of your stuff in there too. I hope that's okay?'

Leaning against the arch of the door beside her, Gabriel gazed at his bride.

Anticipation for what the night would bring had tortured him since he'd seen her on the balcony that morning, and now they were finally alone and all the fantasies that had sustained him through the long wedding banquet, of peeling that sheer dress from her perfect body and then kissing every inch of her soft skin before burying himself in her tight sweetness, could be acted on.

But he would keep his desire in check awhile longer. Even through his fantasies he'd sensed Alessia's nerves growing as the banquet had gone on and guessed the anticipation of their wedding night had got the better of her. It was up to him to help her relax.

'I didn't bring much with me so I'm sure it's all fine,' he assured her with a slow smile. The dressing room, long though it was, *was* small but cleverly designed to maximise every available inch of space. The left-hand side bulged with feminine colour. The right-hand side—his side—had barely a third of the available space taken. 'See, plenty of room.'

She rubbed her arm. 'When will you bring the rest of your stuff?'

'When we move into the stables. In the meantime,

I'll be spending my working weeks in Madrid so will keep the majority of my stuff in my home there.'

Her eyes met his, perfectly plucked eyebrows drawing together. 'I thought you were giving up your business? You said you'd got your affairs in order.'

'No, only my affairs concerning the client I was supposed to start with this week. I will be winding my main business down but I have many other business interests too. There isn't the space for me to work here.'

A flintiness came into the velvet eyes, an edge appearing in her voice. 'I know my quarters are cramped but it's a castle with over three hundred rooms. An office can be created for you without any problem, and it can be as big as you want.'

'It's more convenient to base myself in Madrid— it's easier to travel to the countries I do business in from there,' he explained. 'By the time we move into the stables and the baby's born, my affairs will be much more straightforward and my need to travel much reduced.' Having their child and not having to live in the castle itself should hopefully make living in this royal goldfish bowl more bearable.

The flintiness sharpened. 'That sounds like an excuse to me.'

'It's a truth. The other truth is that I have no wish to live in this castle full-time. There are too many staff to have any real privacy and I suspect that being under this roof means your family and their personal staff will be incentivised to try and change my mind about being a working member of the family. If I'm out of sight then I'm more likely to be out of mind.'

'Is being a working member such an intolerable idea to you?'

'Yes.'

'And you don't think having a husband who spends his working weeks away is an intolerable idea to me?'

'It is only until the renovations are complete.'

'Which could take months.' She raised her chin and gave a smile as flinty as the expression in her eyes. 'I shall come to Madrid with you.'

'That isn't necessary,' he stated as smoothly as he could in an effort to diffuse what his antennae was warning him: that Alessia was spoiling for an argument.

'Why not? Do you have a woman stashed in Madrid waiting for you?'

Surprised at both the question and the tone in which she asked it, he narrowed his eyes. 'Of course not.'

'Then you can have no objection to me travelling there with you.'

Gabriel closed his eyes and inhaled deeply before staring back at the face that now brimmed with what he was coming to recognise as temper. He had no choice but to add fuel to it. 'I'm afraid it's out of the question.'

'Why?'

'Because a circus follows wherever you go, and I have no wish to be a part of it. I've already made that clear.'

'The media circus is not my fault.'

'I am simply stating my reasons.'

'The moment the announcement of our marriage is made public the circus will be on you.'

'But your presence will make it more. The media love you.'

'I don't encourage that.'

'I never said you did, only that I wish to avoid it as much as I can.'

'Then you shouldn't have agreed to marry me. I'm sorry you find the thought of media intrusion so abhorrent but it is possible to have a life as a royal that isn't always accompanied by the flash of cameras, as you will learn for yourself when I accompany you on your travels.'

For the first time, visible anger darkened Gabriel's features but Alessia was too angry at his insinuations about her character and hurt at his readiness to spend the majority of his time apart from her to care about it. 'It's bad enough that I'll be humiliated by a husband who refuses to be my prince even at my own brother's wedding, but I will not be humiliated by a husband who marries me one minute then flies off without me the next too, especially when that wasn't a pre-condition of our marriage, so get used to the idea of having me by your side. If you do have any lovers stashed anywhere, warn them now that you can no longer see them because your wife refuses to be separated from you.' And with that, Alessia snatched a pair of pyjamas off a shelf and stalked into the bathroom, locking the door firmly behind her.

* * *

Alessia had never appreciated how greatly the presence of another could change an atmosphere. Her quarters, her bedroom especially, had been her favourite place in the castle since she was a little girl and would make Marcelo go exploring with her. She truly didn't know what it was that she loved so much about it other than its warm atmosphere—lots of the castle's rooms were cold and unwelcoming to a little girl—but she'd gladly foregone the much larger apartment that could have been hers for it. Gabriel's presence had changed its atmosphere markedly.

They danced cordially around each other as they readied for bed, taking it in turns to use the bathroom, giving each other privacy to undress, and all with fixed, polite smiles that brimmed with a seething undercurrent.

How many brides and grooms argued on their wedding night? she wondered bitterly. Not that they'd argued as such. She doubted Gabriel ever raised his voice. No, Gabriel preferred to make his arguments behind a smooth cordiality she was growing to detest. But she'd seen the anger in his eyes when she'd stood her ground and refused to accept being treated like a chattel. Well, tough. He'd married her. If she had to live in the bed they'd both made then so should he.

Climbing into the bed she'd never shared before, wearing long silk pyjamas with buttons running the length of the top, Alessia leaned her back against the headboard and reached for her book. She always read in bed but tonight was painfully aware she was using her novel as a prop. She imagined that, for Gabriel, sharing a bed with a woman was no big deal. She wished it wasn't a big deal for her too, but apart from the one night they'd shared, this was her first time and her nerves had grown so big that she wasn't sure if they were causing the nausea rampaging in her stomach or if baby hormones were to blame.

When he finally left the bathroom, she took one look at him and her heart juddered, the ripples spreading through her like wildfire. Wearing only a pair of snug black briefs that bulged at the front and accentuated the rugged athleticism of his physique, she doubted Adonis himself could have made a greater impact. She'd seen him entirely naked, of course, but they'd spent that night entwined, and she'd seen him in shorts on the balcony that morning, but the balustrade had hidden much of him. She hadn't had the opportunity to take in everything about him with one sweep of her eyes. All the disparate parts had come together and as he stalked to the bed, eyes softer… and yet more alive…than they'd been when she'd last looked into them, her most intimate parts became molten liquid, and all she could think was that he was the sexiest man to roam the earth or heavens.

The mattress made only the slightest movement as he slipped between the bedsheets but it was movement enough to stop her from breathing. His whispered words from the chapel garden rang in her ear again. *Tonight, I will give you something else to remember this day by.*

She gripped her book harder and pressed the top

of her thighs together as if that could stop the pulsing heat that was spreading from down low in her pelvis.

The thuds of her heart were suddenly deafening.

She sensed his gaze turn to her. Alessia's lungs squeezed so tightly there was no chance of getting air into them even if she could breathe.

This must be the moment that he reached for her and took her in his arms...

A hard scrub of his body had finally cleansed Gabriel of the unwelcome anger inflamed by Alessia's stubborn insistence that she accompany him to Madrid.

Every time she left the castle it was under the flash of camera lenses. He accepted that those flashes and having the press on her heels—having to smile politely and answer their questions—was something she considered a normal part of her life, but she had to accept too that it was not the kind of life he was willing to live. He'd been upfront about it and it was not something he was prepared to compromise on.

But he did accept that he would have to get used to a degree of press intrusion, at least for a short period. As Alessia had rightly pointed out, the moment their marriage was made public, the circus would begin. That didn't mean he had to feed the vultures. A refusal to engage with them or give them anything remotely newsworthy would make the press quickly bore of him.

He doubted the press would ever bore with Alessia. On top of being breathtakingly beautiful and photogenic, she was a style icon to millions. She sold magazines and generated social media clicks by doing nothing but be herself, and, he had to admit, raised great awareness for the charities she patronised as a result.

Staring at her now, he could see from the rigid way she held herself, her clenched jaw and the whites of her knuckles where she held her book, that her anger still lingered. And there was something else in her body language too, there in the tiny tremors of her body... Alessia was as aware of him as he was of her.

Having had enough of the game of silence, Gabriel plucked the book from her hand, then leaned over her to place it on her antique bedside table. He caught the intake of her breath at the same moment the soft fruity scent of Alessia hit his senses.

Had any woman ever smelt so good? Not in his lifetime.

With his back propped against the velvet headboard, he kept his gaze on her until she finally turned her face and those amazing dark velvet eyes locked onto him.

'Let me put your mind at ease,' he said. 'I don't have a lover stashed in Madrid or anywhere. My last relationship ended months ago. I'm strictly monogamous.'

He was rewarded with continued silence.

'And you?' he prompted when she did nothing but gaze into his eyes as if searching for something. 'Are you monogamous too?'

Her teeth grazed her bottom lip. 'I suppose.'

Surprised at her equivocation, he raised a brow.

'Suppose? Surely it's a question that requires only a yes or no answer.'

'Then… Yes.'

Something dark coiled inside him, as unexpected as it was disarming, but he controlled it. 'You don't look certain.'

'I am.'

He stared hard into her brown eyes. His expertise at reading people meant Gabriel knew when someone was lying to him. Alessa was not being truthful. He was certain of it. Which begged the question of why she was lying. As far as he was aware, she'd never been linked to a man so she was discreet in her affairs, probably conducting them all within the castle or in the homes of trusted friends. When it came to cheating, though, he imagined things would get trickier. There were tabloids he knew who would pay a small fortune for a story of Princess Alessia being a love cheat.

If she wasn't a love cheat then why the hesitation about being monogamous? Whatever the answer, the darkness thickened and coiled tighter, and tightened his vocal chords too, and it was a real struggle to keep his voice moderate. 'I don't care what you got up to in your past but I will not accept you taking lovers.' He bore his gaze into hers so there could be no misunderstanding. 'You don't wish to be humiliated by me travelling without you, and I will not suffer the humiliation of being cuckolded. We're married now which means it's you and me, and only you and me. Is that clear?'

Alessia fought the very real urge to laugh. She was quite sure it would come out sounding hysterical.

What would he say if she told him the truth, that he'd been her first? Which incidentally meant he would also be her last.

But how could she tell him that now when she should have told him weeks ago, before things had gone too far between them? How could he forgive her for it? If she hadn't been so inexperienced she would have realised he hadn't put a condom on, but as it was, she'd made the fatal assumption that he'd taken care of things while she'd been in a blissful bubble of sensual feeling. If she'd told him she was a virgin then the subject of contraception would definitely have come up—one thing she knew about her new husband was that he did not leave anything to chance.

If she'd told him she was a virgin he would never have made love to her...

'Are you not going to say anything?' he asked curtly.

Pushing the bedsheets off her lap, she crossed her legs as she twisted to face him. The Ice Man stared back at her, his handsome face expressionless, large hands folded loosely against his taut abdomen. For the beat of a moment the temptation to drag her fingers through the dark hair covering his muscular chest and press down where his heart beat made her skin tingle.

'What do you want me to say?' she asked.

His eyes flashed, but other than that, his expression remained unreadable. 'Whatever's going on in your pretty head would be a start.'

She felt a flare of pleasure at the compliment.

'Trust me, you don't want to know what's in my head.' She linked her fingers together to stop herself, again, from dragging them over his supremely masculine chest. 'But let me put *your* mind at ease—I didn't take my vows lightly. I knew that making them meant I was committing myself to you for the rest of my life, and *only* you.'

His nostrils flared. 'Good.'

'But so we are clear, I am now your wife but that doesn't make me your possession.'

His wife…

'I never said you were.'

'I just wanted to make that clear.'

He leaned forwards, closer to her, a wry expression on his face. 'You did.'

Alessia had no idea why the knots in her belly had loosened so much. If she didn't know better, she would say Gabriel had sounded jealous, but then she reminded herself that if he were, it would only be from a proprietorial sense and not from a place of emotion like her own bout of jealousy had come from that morning.

Grazing her bottom lip, she suddenly blurted out, 'Do you really think I'm pretty?'

He stared at her as if she'd asked the most stupid question in the world. 'Yes.'

'Really?'

He pulled a cynical face. 'I can't be the first man to have told you that.'

'Oh, I've been told I'm pretty by lots of people but

I never know whether to believe them or not.' She shrugged. 'My family are biased, and people like to ingratiate themselves with me. Then there are all the trolls out there who like to tell me that I'm pig ugly, so who knows what I should believe.'

The cynicism vanished. 'You have trolls?'

'Everyone in the public eye has trolls.' She tried not to sound too downbeat about it. If trolls were the worst thing she had to deal with in her privileged life then she had nothing to complain about. 'Nowadays, it comes with the job.'

'Who are these people?'

'Mostly anonymous. It doesn't matter.'

'Of course it matters,' Gabriel disputed roughly. The thought of anyone sitting in front of their phone or computer and targeting Alessia for their poison... He clasped her hand and leaned closer to her, staring straight into the velvet depths. 'Anyone who tells you that you're ugly needs to seek help because you're more than pretty. You're beautiful.'

She stilled, the only movement the widening of her eyes and the parting of her lips as she took a sharp intake of breath. A crawl of colour suffused her cheeks. 'Do you really mean that?' she whispered.

He drew even closer so the tips of their noses almost touched. 'You're beautiful,' he repeated. 'So beautiful that sometimes I look at you and think you must have been created by an enchantment.' And then he did what he'd been aching to do for so long, and tilted his head, brushed his lips to hers and breathed her in.

For the longest time he did nothing but allow his senses to fill with the delicate scent of Alessia's skin. Then he kissed her, gentle sweeping movements that slowly deepened until their lips parted in unison and their tongues entwined in a private dance that sent sensation shooting through him like an electric current through his veins.

All these weeks, Alessia's scent and taste had haunted him, memories so strong he'd come to believe he'd imagined just how intoxicating they were. His memories hadn't lied. Hooking an arm around her waist and pulling her to him, he fed himself on kisses that were as headily addictive and as potent as the strongest aphrodisiac could be.

With a soft sigh, she sank fully into him, returning his hunger with a ravenousness that only fed his burning arousal even more. Tightly she wrapped her arms around his neck, hands and fingers clasping the back of his head, her perfect breasts pressed against his chest, as the passion that had caught them in its grips all those weeks ago cast its tendrils back around them.

From the first whisper of his breath against her lips, Alessia had been reduced to nothing but sensation. The dark taste of Gabriel and the burning thrills of his touch raged through her flesh and veins, feeding the craving for him that she'd carried in every cell of her body since the night they'd...

'No!'

CHAPTER EIGHT

ALESSIA'S MOUTH SHOUTED the word and wrenched away from him before her brain caught up.

Her heart thumping madly, her skin and loins practically screaming their outrage at the severing of such dazzling pleasure, she disentangled herself from his arms and scrambled backwards out of reach.

Stunned eyes followed her movements, Gabriel's breaths coming in short, ragged bursts. 'What's wrong?' he asked hoarsely.

Trying hard to control her own breathing, trying even harder to control the wails of disappointment from her body, Alessia shakily shook her head. 'I can't do this. I'm sorry, but I can't. It's too soon.'

He stared at her in disbelief. 'What are you talking about? How can you say it's too soon when we've just got married?'

'It just is!' she cried, before her lips clamped together and she crossed her arms to hold her biceps, gripping them tightly as protection, not from him but from herself because like the rest of her furious body, her hands were howling to clasp themselves to his cheeks so her equally furious lips could attach themselves back to his mouth, and the whole of her could revel again in the heady delights of Gabriel. Her pelvis felt like it was on fire. Her blood burned. *Everything* burned.

His face contorted and he cursed under his breath before his chest rose as he inhaled deeply, visibly composing himself. 'You have to talk to me,' he said. She could take little comfort that the smoothly controlled voice had a ragged tone to it. 'Tell me what's on your mind. I'm trying to make sense of what you mean about it being too soon when we already know how good we are together. The night we made our child is proof of that.'

'And you walked out the next day without a word of goodbye or even a note,' she retorted tremulously, because it was remembering that little fact that had snapped her out of the sensual haze she'd been caught in.

This time his curse was more audible, and he closed his eyes.

'Are you not going to say anything?' she asked in an attempt to mimic the curt tone he'd used on her earlier, but the upset in her voice was just too strong for it to be successful.

Nausea churned heavily in Gabriel's guts. He'd apologised for not returning her call but the fact of him leaving her sleeping while he slipped out of the room had been left unsaid. He should have known this conversation would one day come.

Arousal still coursed like fire through his loins and

veins, and he closed his eyes again and concentrated on tempering it. Then he locked his stare back on her. 'I left without saying goodbye because when I woke next to you, I felt like the biggest jerk in the world.'

Her chin wobbled but she didn't look away. 'Why?'

'Because your family were generous enough to give me a bed for the night when my plane was grounded and I repaid that generosity by sleeping with their daughter.'

'I'm a twenty-three-year-old woman.'

'But you're not an ordinary woman. You're a princess.'

'I'm also a woman. A woman with feelings, not some mythical creature that can't be hurt.'

'I behaved terribly. I know that. When I woke up… Alessia, I was sickened with myself, not just because of who you are and the abuse of your parents' hospitality but because I never mix business with pleasure. Never.'

Her eyes continued to search his until her neck straightened and something that almost resembled a smile played on her lips. 'You mean I was your first? Mixing of business with pleasure, I mean?'

'Yes.'

Her gaze searched his for a moment more before the smile widened a touch. 'Should I be flattered?'

'If you like.'

'I do like.' Then the smile faded and she stilled again. 'I can understand why you felt bad about yourself for what happened. But, Gabriel, that doesn't excuse or explain your behaviour towards me.'

'It's the truth of it all.'

'Maybe, but it doesn't excuse it. It doesn't. I had the best night of my life with you and then I woke up and you were gone. Do you know how that made me feel?'

He took a long inhale.

'Dirty. I've never…' She swallowed, and drew her knees to her chest and wrapped her arms around them. 'I've never had a one-night stand before. Don't misunderstand me, I didn't fall into your arms expecting any of this—' she waved a hand absently '—to happen, but finding you gone… It hurt. To feel unworthy of even a minute of your time after what we'd shared.'

'I'm sorry,' he said, speaking through a throat that felt like it had razors in it. 'It was never my intention to make you feel like that.'

'Then what was your intention?'

'To get out of Ceres. It felt like I'd woken from a spell and all I could do was kick myself for losing my head the way I did.'

An astuteness came into her stare. 'You don't like losing control of yourself, do you?'

'No,' he agreed.

'Why is that?'

'It's just the way I am.'

She gave a grimacing smile and rubbed her chin against her knees. 'I think we can both agree that what we shared was…madness. A child was created through it and here we are. But I'm sorry, Gabriel, I can't forget how I felt when I realised you'd gone. I kept hoping you sneaked out because you were worried about making love with a princess and my family's reaction if they found out—I guess I was partially right there—so I decided to be a modern woman and call you. I hoped you'd see my message and realise I was just a woman like any other and that there was nothing to stop us seeing each other again, but you blanked me there too, and I can't forget that. I can't forget how cheap you made me feel. I want to put it behind me—I've married you so we're stuck together now—but I've got nothing to replace those feelings with because you're still a stranger to me, and until you start opening up about who you really are, you'll continue to be a stranger.'

Alessia's heart was beating hard. Her body was still furious with her for severing the passionate connection with Gabriel and, though she knew she'd done the right thing in not letting things go any further, the ache deep inside was a taunt that she was being a prideful fool.

She didn't think she'd ever been so honest about her feelings before. 'Never complain and never explain' was a creed many royal families lived by and it was a creed she'd taken to heart at a very young age. The only person she'd ever felt able to open up to was her brother Marcelo, and even then she'd often held back because he'd suffered for being who he was born to be far more than she ever had. Alessia had never yearned to be someone else like him.

In many ways, laying her cards on the table was liberating, and she experienced a little jolt to realise that there was something in Gabriel that put her at ease enough to say what was on her mind and in her heart without sanitising or editing. There was another jolt to realise that when she was with him, she didn't have to *be* a princess. And it wasn't just about him bringing out the woman beneath the princess mask—for Gabriel, the mask dropped itself of its own accord.

And then she remembered, again, keeping her virginity from him and another spasm of guilt cut through her.

It shouldn't matter, she knew that. Her sexual history—or lack of it—was no one's business but her own. It shouldn't matter, but she suspected that for Gabriel it would.

After the longest passage of silence had passed, hands more than twice the size of hers wrapped around her fingers.

'I can see I have much to do to make amends,' he said, his expression as serious as his tone, 'and I will do my best to do that. There is much to learn about each other, but I should warn you, I'm not one for baring my soul. I have always been a private person.'

'Would you believe it, but I'm not one for baring my soul either?' She gave a rueful shrug. 'Not usually, in any case.' And then she shook her head as if disbelieving. 'And yet I cried in your arms and told you everything I was feeling that night because on some level I must have trusted you.'

It was the first time Alessia had considered that. Though there had been no forethought behind it, she'd trusted Gabriel with her feelings as well as with her body that night. She'd unbuttoned herself to him like she'd never done with anyone else on this earth, and then he'd left her life as if he'd never been in it. Was it any wonder she was so scared of getting close to him again?

The look on Gabriel's face as another long stretch of time passed told her he was thinking the same thoughts.

'Yes,' he finally said. 'I think I do believe that, and I will do whatever it takes to rebuild your trust in me.' Then he released her hands and lifted the bedsheet for her. In a softer tone, he said, 'It is late. We should get some sleep.'

She hesitated. Should she sleep in the guest room? Insist he sleep in it?

But the expression in his gaze was steady. Reassuring. And it made her mind up for her.

Her heart in her throat, Alessia slipped back under the sheets while Gabriel leaned over to turn out the lights, then her heart almost shot out of her ribs when he reached for her.

'I'm just going to hold you,' he murmured, and pulled her rigid body to him. Then, having manoeuvred her as easily as if he were manipulating play dough so that her cheek was pressed into his chest and their arms wrapped around each other, he dropped a kiss into her hair. 'Goodnight, wife.'

'Goodnight, husband,' she whispered.

The moment Alessia awoke, her eyes pinged open. There was an arm draped over her waist, the attached hand loose against her belly. A knee rested in the back of her calf.

The duskiness of the room told her the sun had already risen.

From Gabriel's steady, rhythmic breathing, he was in deep sleep.

She had no idea how long she lay there, afraid to move so much as a muscle. Afraid of the feelings swirling inside her. The deep yearn to wriggle back into his solid body and press herself to him. To wake him…

Holding her breath, she slowly inched herself out from under his arm. Once she'd inched herself off the bed too, she carefully picked up her book and her phone, and crept out of the room. Only when the door was closed behind her was she able to breathe.

Downstairs, she padded into the kitchen and fixed herself a coffee. It was the one thing she liked to do for herself, and when she had days without any engagements, she relished the solitude and independence the early mornings gave her. The days she had engagements, staff surrounded her before she'd even climbed out of bed.

Her hand clenched around her favourite coffee mug, and she squeezed her eyes shut. Hurt and anger had made her tell Gabriel she would accompany him to Madrid. She wondered if he would even pretend not to be relieved when she told him that wouldn't be possible after all?

Rolling her neck, she pulled herself together and took her coffee into the day room, opened the curtains, snuggled into her reading chair and opened the book.

Ten minutes later and she was still on the same page. It didn't matter how many times she read the same passage, the words refused to penetrate. Or should that be, her brain refused to concentrate?

With a sigh, she closed her eyes.

Her brain refused to concentrate because it wanted to think about Gabriel, and nothing but Gabriel.

Wasn't it enough that her stupid brain had taken for ever to go to sleep because Gabriel's arms had been around her and her every inhalation had breathed in the divine scent of his skin? Wasn't it enough that her body had also taken for ever to relax itself into sleep for the exact same reason? She swore it had taken at least an hour before she'd even been able to breathe properly. And then there were all the thoughts that had crowded her already frazzled mind, every single one about Gabriel, never mind the battle between her mind and her rigid yet aching body. That had been the worst of it. That yearning ache deep inside her that had spent hours begging her to wake him with a kiss.

'You're up early.'

If Alessia hadn't already finished her coffee she would have spilt the contents of her mug, which was still in her hand, all over herself.

Snapping her eyes open, she turned her head and found Gabriel in the doorway looking at her with an expression that made her heart inflate and her belly flip.

Black hair mussed, his jaw and neck thick with

stubble, all he wore was a pair of low-slung black jeans that perfectly showed off the muscular chest her face had spent half the night pressed against, and the yearning that had kept her awake for hours hit her with its full force.

The hint of a smile played on his mouth. 'What does a man do for coffee here?'

Her certainty that he could sense or see the effect he was having on her sent a flush of heat thrashing through her, and she had to clear her throat to speak. 'There's a pot made in the kitchen.' Trying not to cringe at the overt croak in her voice, she straightened her back and added, 'If you're hungry, press three on any landline and it will connect you to the palace kitchen. The chefs will make you anything you want.'

The only thing I want is you, Gabriel thought. Although the angle of Alessia's armchair hid much of her from his sight, the little he could see was enough to make his chest tighten and his pulses surge. That his appearance had such a visible effect on her only heightened the sensations, and he ground his feet into the carpet and filled his lungs slowly before speaking again. 'Have you eaten?'

She tucked a strand of her silky dark hair behind an ear. 'Not yet. I'll order something later, but please, don't wait for me. The chefs are used to preparing dishes any time of the day or night.'

'I'll wait until you eat. Did you want another coffee?'

'No, thank you. I'm limiting myself to one a day.' She pressed her belly as explanation.

The tightness in his chest loosened and expanded, and he nodded his understanding. 'Can I get you anything else?'

'No. But thank you.'

Gabriel nodded again and turned down the corridor that led to the kitchen. The aroma of freshly ground coffee greeted him, and he poured himself a cup and added a heaped spoonful of sugar while taking a moment to gather himself together.

He'd fallen asleep surprisingly easily considering everything, but had woken with a weighty feeling in the pit of his stomach. He'd felt Alessia's absence from the bed at the same moment everything that had occurred between them on their wedding night had flashed through his mind. The weighty feeling had spread to his chest as, for the first time, he had an insight into how she must have felt that morning to find him gone.

Why had he never allowed himself to think of that before? He didn't have the answer. He'd always acknowledged to himself that his behaviour that morning had been abhorrent but all the justifications he'd heaped on himself had smothered his ability to think of how it must have been for Alessia.

He wished he could say that she was overreacting. One-night stands happened all the time. Alessia wasn't his first and, princess though she was, she was a modern woman so he doubted he was hers either—although her reaction to his question about monogamy and his reaction to that reaction told him previous relationships were a subject best avoided between them—but what they'd shared did *not* happen all the time. The chemistry between them had been off the charts.

It still was.

That Alessia refused to act on the chemistry was a situation of his own making. It was on him to make things right.

Carrying his coffee back to the main living area, he took a seat on the armchair closest to her. Her eyes flickered up from the book she was reading, colour rising on her cheeks.

'I would like us to take a visit to the stables at some point this weekend,' he said. 'We need to start thinking about how we want it to be renovated.'

'Sure.' She closed her book. 'I'll ask Ena—my private secretary—to find the keys for us. She'll be at her desk in an hour.'

'What about your domestic staff? What time do they start?' All the times he'd been at the castle, whatever the time, the stone walls had contained a hive of activity, worker bees efficiently getting on with their individual tasks, unobtrusive but always in the background.

'This is an official day off for me so they won't come until I call for them.'

'Do you have many free days?'

'My weekends are normally free, but sometimes I have engagements to attend, sometimes issues crop up that need to be dealt with—my role within the family isn't something I can turn on and off. None of us can.'

'How many engagements do you go to each week?'

'It varies.'

'What do you like to do in your free time?'

Alessia studied him warily before answering. All this talk about engagements made her think there was a real irony in Gabriel making the effort to engage with her as he was currently doing when she'd been the driving force on their night together, forcing him to engage in conversation with her. She remembered thinking that he didn't seem to like her. Clearly he'd wanted her but that was physical desire. It was the liking of *her*, her personality, she'd had doubts about. She still had them. For all his excuses about ghosting her, she couldn't help but think that if he'd liked her more, he would have returned her call.

She wished she didn't feel so resentful that he was only making this effort to engage and get to know her now as part of his efforts to build trust between them so they could have some kind of harmony in their marriage rather than because he wanted to know her for her own sake as she'd so longed to know him.

But there was no point thinking like this. She had to think of their marriage as being like her headmistress's proverbial bed and imagine it having a lumpy mattress. Alessia had no choice but to lie on it and play her part in flattening those lumps, and as she thought that, she was helpless to stop the image of them naked, entwined together on a real bed, and helpless to stop another wave of longing.

She expelled a slow breath and forced herself to answer. 'Sometimes I see friends. Sometimes I go

shopping. Sometimes I'll spend a whole day reading or watching boxsets. It depends.' And then, because she knew she *had* to get over her resentment
and find a way to deal with her hurt otherwise she'd
be condemning them both to a lifetime of misery,
added, 'What about you? What do you do on your
days off?'

'I don't take many days off but when I have free
time I like to unwind with a bourbon and a good film
or a book.' He nodded at the book on her lap. 'What
are you reading?'

Bracing herself for a cutting comment, Alessia
showed him the cover. It was a historical romance,
the kind of book her brothers had always laughed at
her for enjoying.

Gabriel didn't seem to find anything amusing
about her literary choice, pulling a musing face and
asking, 'Any good?'

'So far.'

'Do you read only historical books?'

'I'll read anything.'

'Me too, although I tend to lean towards thrillers
and biographies. I have a library at my home in Madrid. I'm sure you'll find something on the shelves
you'll enjoy.'

Caution made her reluctant to jump to conclu-
sions. 'Does that mean you're going to let me come
with you?'

'I don't remember you giving me any choice in the
matter,' he said dryly. 'But you're right, I didn't make
it a precondition of our marriage and, having thought

about it, it would be good for you to see the place I call home. All I ask is that your presence there is kept from the press. I am serious about my privacy, Alessia, and would like any press intrusion to be kept to an absolute minimum.'

So he didn't actually want her to come. Like this whole conversation, it was a sop to her.

She lifted her chin, determined not to show the hurt. 'Our press office only notifies the press about my movements for official engagements so that won't be a problem.'

'Good.'

'But if it does become a problem, I'm sure you'll be glad to know I'll only be able to travel with you next week. After that, I'm afraid my engagement diary's full, so you will get your wish to have me out of your hair Mondays to Fridays after all. Now, if you'll excuse me, I'm going to do my dance exercises and take a shower.' Already regretting the flash of bitterness she'd had no control over, Alessia rose from her chair and, in a softer tone, added, 'Order yourself some breakfast—please, don't go hungry on my account.'

Before she could walk away, though, he said, 'Have you heard of Monica Binoche?'

She turned her face back to him. 'The French actress?' Monica Binoche was the actress Marcelo had had a crush on in his early teenage years. Alessia distinctly remembered him asking their father if she could be invited to castle so he could meet her, and their father laughing and replying with something along the lines of 'If only.'

'Yes.' Gabriel took a deep breath, and watched her reaction closely as he said, 'She's my mother.'

CHAPTER NINE

ALESSIA'S MOUTH DROPPED OPEN, her eyes widening in shock.

'Monica Binoche is my mother and the reason I value my privacy so highly,' Gabriel explained evenly. 'My father was Pedro Gonzalez. You probably haven't heard of him but he was a well-respected acting agent. He died in his sleep five years ago. Heart failure.'

She sat back on her armchair, her face expressing nothing but compassion. 'That's awful. I'm so sorry.'

He smiled grimly. 'Thank you. It was not unexpected. He was seventy-eight and not in good health. I loved him, I miss him, but it's my mother I want to talk to you about.'

He'd never discussed either of his parents with anyone but his sister in his entire adult life other than in generic terms, but Alessia wanted to know who he was and why, and until she knew, she would never trust him. He could see too that she deserved to know his past so she could understand that his refusal to play the royal media game was not anything personal or a slight against her or her family.

'There is nothing my mother enjoys more than attention,' he said. 'It's what feeds her. As children, my sister and I were accessories to her. I don't mean to paint her as a bad mother—she tried her best—but she thought nothing of using Mariella and I as props for photo opportunities. For my mother, it's a terrible day if she leaves the house and there isn't a swarm of paparazzi waiting on the doorstep. I used to have to fight my way through them just to go to school. On quiet celebrity news days, they would sometimes wait outside the school gate for us.'

'But I thought France had strict privacy laws?'

'It does. Much stricter than what you have here in Ceres. What you're not taking into consideration is that my mother encouraged it. She wanted her privacy invaded. It's how she found validation—how she still finds it.'

'That must have been rough for you,' she said softly.

'It was infuriating. And it was the reason I didn't invite her to our wedding. She hasn't used me as an accessory in twenty years, not since I gave her the ultimatum, but I didn't want to put temptation in her way. Inviting her to a royal wedding, no matter how small it was, and expecting her not to put it on her social media feeds would be like locking a recovering alcoholic in a fully stocked English pub.'

Her eyes hadn't left his face since he'd started his explanation. 'What was the ultimatum you gave her?'

'That either she stopped using Mariella and me as props for her ego or we'd move in full-time with our father.' He gave a wry smile. 'See? She does love us in her own way because it all stopped right then.'

'Your parents divorced?'

'They separated when I was twelve.'

'Because of your mother's behaviour?'

He laughed. 'His behaviour wasn't much better. My father was her agent and credited himself with ensuring her big break. As her fame grew, his jealousy grew and he started having affairs, I think to validate himself and to humiliate her. He wasn't very discreet about it. He was thirty years older than her screwing around like a teenager. She was an aging ingenue terrified of the aging process and being thought irrelevant. It was a toxic combination that eventually turned into warfare between them. Both of them blamed the other for the destruction of their marriage and both refused to move out of the marital home or give an inch on custody of me and Mariella. Neither of them was prepared to give an inch on anything.'

Alessia's head was reeling. Whatever could be said about her own childhood and upbringing, the security of her parents' marriage had never been in doubt. She'd rarely heard them exchange a cross word. 'That must have been tough to live with.'

'It was. They both tried hard to be good parents to us but there were a few years when they were too wrapped up in their mutual loathing to notice the damage they were doing.'

'What made them see sense?'

'Me.'

'You?'

He inclined his head. 'I'd listened to so many of their screaming matches that I knew exactly what their issues with each other were and what they both wanted, so I sat them down individually and brokered peace negotiations.'

'You did? When you were *twelve*?' At twelve, the only brokering Alessia had done was when trying, unsuccessfully, to negotiate the right to read books with rather more salacious material than her Enid Blyton's.

'I was fourteen at this point. It took a couple of weeks of negotiating between them but eventually they agreed to sell the house and split the profits.' He flashed a quick grin. 'That way, neither of them "won." I also got them to agree to buy a new home each within a mile of mine and Mariella's school, and drew up a custody plan that gave them equal access to us.'

'How did that work?'

'There's fifty-two weeks in a year. We spent twenty-six with each parent, with each year carefully planned to cater for their individual work schedules. We alternated Christmases and birthdays.'

'A fair compromise to them both,' she mused dubiously.

'Exactly. Neither won. Neither lost.'

'What about you and your sister, though? Wasn't it hard carving up your time between them and never being settled in one home?'

'That brought its own challenges but it was easier than living in a war zone. I also had it written into the contracts that they were forbidden from bad-mouthing each other to us.'

She rubbed the back of her head. 'You were one mature teenager.'

'My mother used to say I was born serious.'

Her eyes were searching. 'Do you agree with her? Or was it circumstances that made you that way?'

He considered this. 'A combination of both, perhaps. The circumstances certainly made me the man I am today. Pursuing a career in diplomacy felt natural after negotiating their divorce and custody arrangements.'

'And the circumstances gave you a pathological loathing of the press?' And, Alessia suspected, a loathing for conflict and a need to always be firmly in control of himself and his surroundings.

He nodded. 'I changed my surname legally when I turned eighteen—my father's name isn't as well-known as my mother's but their marriage made him a celebrity in his own right. I value my privacy because I never had it when I was a child.'

'And now you've married a princess,' she said quietly, now understanding why he was so adamant in his refusal to be a 'proper' royal. 'A life you never wanted.'

He shifted forwards in his seat and stared deep into her eyes. 'I married *you*, Alessia, and I need you to understand that though I don't want the princess, I do want the woman. I want *you*.'

So many emotions filled her at the sincerely delivered words that she couldn't even begin to dissect them. It frightened her how desperately she longed to believe him, believe that he did want her, but even that longing was fraught because she didn't know if he meant he wanted her, body, heart and soul, or just the first part, and she couldn't bring herself to ask because she didn't know if she'd be able to take the answer.

She was saved from her tortured thoughts by the ringing of the bell and the simultaneous trilling of both their phones, but there was no relief in the interruption, only a plunge in her heart as she immediately understood what it meant. It meant the media circus Gabriel so despised and had spent his adult life avoiding had come for him.

She closed her eyes briefly and sighed. 'I think the announcement of our marriage has just gone out.'

It took three days before Gabriel and Alessia were able to inspect the place that was going to be their marital home. Gabriel had expected news of their marriage to cause a sensation but, when it broke, sensation was an understatement. The east side of the castle, the half open to tourists, was so besieged by press that it had to close to visitors. The rotors of helicopters ignoring the no-fly zone above the castle was a constant noise for hours until the Ceres military put a stop to their illegality. Gabriel's phones, business and personal, didn't stop ringing. It seemed that everyone he'd ever been acquainted with felt the need to call and congratulate him. Once the press obtained his number, he'd had enough and turned it off, but not before his mother, furious not to have been invited to the wedding, cried and wailed down the phone like the good actress she was for an hour before ringing off so she could call his sister, who'd stayed for the wedding night in the castle's guest quarters, and sob theatrically down the phone to her. Alessia's phone rang non-stop too, her private secretary and other clerical staff rushing in and out of their quarters with updates and messages, the usual buzz of activity within the castle walls having turned into a loud hum.

He'd not needed to step foot out of the castle grounds to feel the impact of the circus.

Gabriel knew the stables, which had once housed hundreds of horses, had initially been converted for the reigning queen's mother to live in, but it was still much, *much* bigger than he'd expected. U-shaped with a bell tower in its centre, it was built with the same sand-coloured stone as the rest of the castle, its roof the same terracotta hue that topped the castle's turrets, and was situated close to the side of the castle where the Berruti family lived and worked but far enough from it to feel entirely separate. Even before Alessia unlocked the grand front door, he knew this would make the perfect home for them.

And then he stepped inside and knew it would only make the perfect home if the entire thing was stripped to bare walls and started again. The high-ceilinged reception room they'd stepped into glowered—there was no other word for it—with faded glamour. It was a glamour that would have held no appeal even if it wasn't faded. Nothing had been done to mitigate the lack of natural light coming in from the small windows. If anything, the décor had been chosen to enhance the shadows. Even the exquisite paintings that lined the reception walls seemed to have been selected for the menace they exuded, and he recognised a variation of Judith with the severed head of Holofernes.

Not wanting to insult Alessia, he kept his initial impression to himself and indicated the tall archway in front of them. 'Do you want to lead the way?'

Having been staring wordlessly at a painting of the medusa turning naked men into stone, Alessia faced him, her brow creased in confusion.

'Do you want to give me the grand tour?' he elaborated.

'But I can't—I've never been in here before.'

He gazed into her velvet eyes, convinced she was joking. 'You never visited your grandmother, who lived on the same estate as you? But I thought she only died eight years ago?'

'She did but she was a miserable witch who hated people and *really* hated children.'

'That explains the décor then,' he murmured.

A glint of humour flickered over her face and then she put a hand to her mouth and giggled. 'It's *awful*, isn't it?' She shook her head, her giggles turning into a peal of laughter. 'Marcelo told me it was bad but I never guessed it was this bad. I'm glad she never let me visit. This would have given me nightmares.'

The weight in his chest lifting at the sight of Alessia with glee etched over her beautiful face and the sound of her husky laughter ringing in his ears, Gabriel couldn't stop his own amusement escaping. In his laughter was a huge dose of relief.

Since the statement had been released, Alessia had carried herself with a careful deportment around him. She was unerringly polite but meticulous about not touching him... Not until they went to bed. The moment the light went out, she would wrap her arms around him under the bedsheets and press her face to his bare chest just as they'd done on their wedding night. But, as on their wedding night, she held herself rigidly, barely drawing a breath. He could feel the fight she was waging with herself, the rapid beats of her heart a pulse against his skin, but knew better than to do anything more than hold her. As painful as it was to accept, he'd hurt her deeply. He couldn't wipe that hurt out with confidences about his childhood. She needed to learn to trust him.

And so he would lie there with her, under the sheets, her beautiful body entwined with his, holding himself back from even stroking her hair, hardly able to breathe himself with the pain of his desire cramping his lungs, having to push out the memories of the first time they'd laid entwined, both naked, fitting together like a jigsaw. When he did manage to push aside images that only fired the desire he was having to suppress, his thoughts never strayed from her. The more time he spent with her, the greater his thirst to know everything there was to know about the woman behind the always smiling, dutiful princess who so rarely smiled for him.

So to see her now, her face alight with the joy of shared absurdity, her laughter still filling his senses…

'Do you think she put these paintings here to repel people from going any further than the front door?' he asked, ramming his hands into his pockets to stop them from reaching for her.

God knew how badly he longed to reach for her.

'I'd put money on it.'

'She hated people that much?'

'More.'

'How on earth did she cope with royal life if she hated people?'

'By drinking copious amounts of gin. As soon as my mother took the throne after my grandfather's death, my grandmother announced she never wanted to endure another royal engagement or the company of another human ever again and insisted the stables be converted into a home for her. When she moved in she demanded—in all seriousness—that her new household be staffed only by mutes.' But relating this only set Alessia's laughter off again as the ridiculousness of her grandmother's behaviour really hit home, which in turn set Gabriel's laughter off again too.

Feeling lighter than she'd done in a long time—it *was* true that laughter was good for the soul—Alessia wiped the tears from her eyes. 'Come on,' she said, 'let's go and see if we can find her potion room.'

The pair of them were still sniggering when they went under the arch and entered a rectangular room with cantilevered stairs ascending from the centre.

The posts at the bottom of each gold railing were topped with a gargoyle's head.

'They can go,' Alessia said, shuddering at the ugly things.

'The whole lot can go. Shall we start from the top or the bottom?'

'Let's start at the top and then we can save the dungeon for a treat at the end of it all.'

He laughed again.

He had a great laugh, she thought dreamily, a great rumble that came from deep inside him and was expelled with the whole of his body. When he laughed… Just as when he smiled, creases appeared around his eyes, deep lines grooving along the sides his mouth… Just as when he smiled, it did something to her.

She hadn't laughed like that with anyone since her school days.

'Did you have much to do with her?' he asked.

'Not really, thank God. I was six when my grandfather died so I don't have many solid memories of her before that. She would terrorise us at Christmas, Easter and family birthdays when my mother forced her to join us for celebration meals but that was the extent of my interaction with her…apart from the time when Marcelo and I were playing tennis and the ball went into what was considered to be her garden, and she chased me off like I was trespasser.'

Stepping through the first door they came to on the landing, Alessia was relieved that the worst thing about the bedroom was the blood-red wallpaper. It was replicated in all the other rooms, including the master bedroom. As she peered into the adjoining dressing room, a walled mirror reflected the four-poster bed back at her and her heart jolted to know that this suite would be the room she would share with Gabriel for the rest of her life, and as she thought this, he appeared in the reflection and their eyes met.

He stood stock-still.

The force of the jolt her heart made this time almost punched it out of her.

For a long moment, they did nothing but stare at each other. The longer she gazed at his reflection, the more the deep reds and shadows of the room reflected in the angles of his handsome face and the black clothes he wore, giving him a vampiric quality that sent a thrill rushing through her veins and dissolved the lingering humour that had bound them together in a way she had never expected.

She wanted him so badly…

Oh, why was she still resisting? Gabriel was her husband and she was his wife and that meant something.

Because you're still frightened.

Gabriel's confiding in her about his childhood and his parents' divorce had helped Alessia understand him better but it hadn't changed the deep-rooted instinct to protect herself. If anything it had made it stronger because sympathy and empathy had softened her even more towards him.

He took a step towards her.

A pulse throbbed deep in her pelvis.

The battle between her head, her heart and her

body, between the princess and the woman, had been an impossible war to manage since they'd agreed to marry.

With each hour that passed, her longing for him grew stronger. When the lights went out, her weakness for him almost gobbled her up, and she would lay enveloped in his arms, breathing in his glorious scent, desire filling her from the roots of her hair to the tips of her toes, torturing herself; torturing them both because she could feel Gabriel's suppressed desire as deeply as she felt her own, which only made things worse.

She was torturing them both.

He took another step closer.

Blood roared in her head.

One more step.

She blinked and there he was, right behind her, towering over her just like a vampire from the films.

The beats of her heart tripled in an instant.

Not an inch of his body touched hers but he stood close enough for her skin to tingle with sensation.

'I don't know about you,' he murmured, 'but I think we should knock through the adjoining room. Create another dressing room and double the size of the bathroom.'

It was only when Alessia snatched a breath to answer that she realised she'd been holding it. 'That... Sorry, what did you say?'

His lips twitched but those amazing kaleidoscopic eyes didn't leave hers. He placed his mouth to the back of her ear. 'That we should double the size of our bathroom.'

His mouth didn't make contact but his breath did. It danced through her hair and over her lobe, and then entered her skin like a pulse of electricity that almost knocked her off her feet.

His eyes glimmered. 'Let's see what delights the ground floor has for us.' And then he turned and strolled out of the dressing room as if nothing had just passed between them.

It took a few beats for Alessia to pull her weak legs together.

Where she had to hold the banister to support her wobbly frame, Gabriel sauntered down the stairs with such nonchalance that she wondered if she'd just imagined the hooded pulse in his eyes and the sensuality in his voice.

And then he reached the bottom of the stairs and turned his gaze back to her, and she saw it again. His unashamed hunger for her.

CHAPTER TEN

LATER THAT EVENING, having showered and changed for dinner, Alessia found Gabriel in the dining room. The table had been set for their meal but he was sat at the other end surrounded by sheets of paper.

He looked up as she entered the room. His gaze flickered over her and she caught again that flash of desire as another smile that creased his eyes lit his handsome face.

The longing that had caught her in her grandmother's dressing room flooded her limbs again, weakening them, and it took a beat before she could close the door and cross the room to stand beside him.

'What are you doing?' she asked, glad that her voice, at least, still sounded normal. The rest of her had felt decidedly abnormal since her grandmother's dressing room, like electricity had replaced the blood in her veins. She'd been aware of every movement and every sensation her body made, from the lace knickers she'd pulled up her legs and over her thighs, to the lipstick she'd held between her fingers and applied to lips that tingled, to the perfume she'd dabbed to the pulses on her neck and wrists. Every whisper of sound she heard outside the bedroom had made her heart leap.

It was pounding now, as hard as she'd ever known it.

Why was she standing so close to him?

He looked her up and down again, this time much more slowly. His nostrils flared. 'Getting some ideas down about what we can do with the stables while the ideas are fresh in my mind. I'd like to have my office facing the garden on the ground floor.'

Her arm brushing against his, Alessia peered at the sheets. He'd sketched the floor plan in remarkable detail. How could he remember it so clearly? she wondered, awed too at how well he'd recalled the proportions of each room.

Why this should make her heart swell and ripple even more she couldn't begin to guess.

And why she'd leaned so close into him she couldn't begin to guess either.

Trying hard to cover the emotions thrashing through her, Alessia shifted away from him then turned round so her back was to the table, raised herself onto her toes and used her hands as purchase to lift herself onto it.

They were almost eye level.

If she moved her foot an inch to the left, it would brush against the calf of his leg.

'You are keen to get out of the castle,' she managed to tease. Or tried. She couldn't seem to breathe properly.

His eyes locked onto hers. 'I don't like my business belonging to everyone else.'

Somewhere in the dim recess of her mind, she understood what he meant. The family's personal wing of the castle was busy. Alessia had her own offices but they tended to blur with her private quarters, clerical as well as domestic staff in and out, her family's clerical staff often popping in to ask her questions or get her input. Everything was fluid, communication between the family's respective teams high, everyone working and pulling together for the same aim—the monarchy's success.

Right then, she couldn't have cared less about the monarchy's success. Right then, the only thing Alessia could focus on was the hooded desire flowing from Gabriel's eyes, entwining with the buzz in her veins, and the feel of his calf beneath her toes...

Large hands gripped the bottom of her thighs just above the knees. Jaw clenched, Gabriel brought his face close to hers and bore his gaze into her. 'What are you doing, Lessie?'

'I don't know,' she whispered, staring right back at him.

Had *she* kicked her shoes off so she could rub her toes against his leg?

Her head was swimming. She knew she should push his hands away but the sensations and heat licking her from the outside in were too strong. Erotic fantasies were filling her, a yearn for Gabriel's strong fingers to dip below the hem of her white, floaty skirt and slide up her thighs to where the heat throbbed the most.

Another image filled her: Gabriel lifting the strawberry-coloured bandeau top she'd paired the skirt with over her breasts and taking her nipples into his mouth.

Was that why she'd chosen to wear a top that needed no bra? she wondered hazily.

'Alessia, talk to me.'

His voice was thick, and as she gazed helplessly into his eyes, the pupils swirled and pulsed into black holes she could feel herself being pulled into.

'I... I don't want to talk,' she whispered hoarsely, unable to stop herself falling into the limitless depths.

Gabriel tightened his grip on Alessia's thighs and tried his damnedest to tighten his control. He could feel her desire with all of his senses, feeding the thick arousal that had become a living part of him, unleashing unbound since she'd walked into the dining room, as beautiful and as sexy a sight as he had ever seen. The heat of her quivering skin burned into his flesh, its scent sinking into his airwaves. Hunger, pure, unfiltered, flashed from her melting velvet eyes into his. It was there too in the breathless pitch of her husky voice. Smouldering.

God, he wanted her, with every fibre of his being, but he would not be the one to make the first move. It had to come from her.

He drew his face even closer to hers and forced the words out. 'Alessia, what do you want?'

Her hands suddenly clasped his cheeks. Her breaths coming in short, ragged bursts, the minty taste of her warm breath flowed into his senses, making him grip even tighter as desire throbbed and burned its way relentlessly through him.

It was the control she could see him hanging onto by a thread that unlocked the last of Alessia's mental chain. She could feel Gabriel's hunger for her as deeply as she felt her own but he chose to starve than do anything without her explicit, wholehearted consent because he knew the mental agonies she'd been going through and, more importantly, he understood them.

He would rather put himself through the agony of denial than risk hurting her again, and her heart filled with such emotion it felt like it could burst out of her.

It was impossible to secure her heart against him. *Impossible.* Her heart and her body were intricately linked when it came to Gabriel and if she couldn't give one without the other then so be it. She'd committed herself to him for life, and the feelings he evoked in her were never going to subside.

What was the point in fighting the woman inside her any longer?

She was crazy for him.

Gazing deep into his eyes, she whispered, 'I want you.'

He breathed in deeply and shuddered.

'I want you,' she repeated, and then she could hold back no more and, digging the tips of her fingers into his cheeks, she kissed him with every ounce of the passion she'd been denying them.

The groan that came with his response could have been a roar.

In seconds he was off his seat, holding her tightly

to him and kissing her back with a ferocity that sent her head spinning.

As if he'd looked inside her head and read her fantasies, long fingers dipped under her skirt and dragged up her thigh, and round to clasp her bottom.

Arms entwined around his neck, she closed off the world and sank into her senses…senses which were receptacles for Gabriel, for his taste, his touch… All of him.

Lips moving together, tongues duelling, fingers scraped over flesh and ripped and pulled at the intrusive fabric separating them. Grabbing his shirt to loosen it, she fumbled with the buttons before giving up and slipping her hand beneath it, flattening her palm against his hard abdomen, thrilling at the heat of his skin, the soft hair covering the smoothness. Up her hands splayed, ruching his shirt as her fingers rose until he broke the connection of their mouths to undo the top few buttons himself and yank it over his head.

Gabriel would not have believed it possible for his arousal to deepen any further but then he saw the drugged ringing of Alessia's eyes as she wantonly grazed her stare over his chest. When she put her mouth to his nipple and scraped her nails over his back, the charge that fired through his veins…

Never had he responded with such violent fever…

Apart from with Alessia.

Time had dimmed the intensity of the pleasure they'd shared that night but now, with her rosebud lips worshipping him and her hands stroking and scraping over his burning flesh, he knew that dimming had been an essential defence mechanism in him because the force of his desire was too savage and greedy to be unleashed again.

But it was unleashed now. Unleashed and frenzied and as essential as the air he breathed. *She* was as essential to him as the air he breathed, and he wanted to taste every part of her and consume her into his being.

Clasping her hair he used every ounce of his control to gently pull her head back.

Those drugged velvet eyes met his. Colour slashed her cheeks, her lips, lipstick kissed off, the darkest he'd ever seen them. He kissed them again. Hard. Thoroughly. And then he buried his mouth into her neck and pressed her down so she was laid on the table, her legs hooked around his waist, and set about consuming her.

Alessia was lost in a world of delirious pleasure. Her flesh burned and, deep inside her, pulses were converging and thickening, an urgency building that Gabriel's slavish assault only added fuel to. Her bandeau top yanked down, she cried out when his hot mouth covered her breast: sucking, biting, licking, sending her spinning until she cried out again and arched her back when he moved to the other.

The assault of his mouth continued down to her belly, his hands clasping her skirt and pushing it up to her hips. Raising his face to look at her with hooded, passion-ridden eyes, he bared his teeth with a growl and clasped her knickers. With another growl, he tugged them down her thighs and off her legs, and in moments he was on his knees with his face buried in the most feminine part of her.

This was a pleasure like no other, an all-consuming barrage of stimulation, and, closing her eyes tightly, Alessia lost herself in the flames.

The musky scent and taste of Alessia's swollen sex was the most potent aphrodisiac to Gabriel's senses. She opened herself to him like a flower in full bloom, her thighs around his neck, and with a greed he'd never known he possessed, he devoured the sweet nectar of her desire, moving his tongue rhythmically over the core of her pleasure until she stiffened beneath him and then, with shudders that rippled through her entire body, and the heels of her feet kicking him, cried her pleasure in one long, continuous moan.

Close to losing his head with the strength of his arousal, Gabriel only just managed to hold onto his control until the shudders wracking her had subsided and her moans turned into a breathless sigh of fulfilment.

Rising back to his feet, he gazed down at her pleasure-saturated face and then he could hold on no more. Working quickly at his trousers, he tugged them down with his underwear and finally let his erection spring free. The urgency to be inside her had him gripping her hips so her bottom was at the edge of the table, and then he guided himself to the place he most desperately wanted to be. And then with one long drive, he buried himself deep inside her slick tightness.

It was Gabriel's groan as he drove himself inside her that added a spark to the kindling of Alessia's spent desire. Her climax had been so powerful it had sapped all the energy that had driven her to that most glorious of peaks. It was the way his glazed eyes fixed on her as he thrust into her a second time that added fuel to the steadily increasing heat. And it was when he raised her thighs for deeper penetration and his groin rubbed against her still-throbbing nub that the flames caught all over again.

Oh, my God…

It wasn't Gabriel making love to her. It was an animal who pinned her hands to the sides of her head and laced his fingers through hers, an animal who drove so hard and so furiously into her, feeding the flames of her desire… And yet Gabriel *was* there too. He was there, behind those glazed eyes.

This animal…this beast…this was Gabriel in all his raw beauty.

She could see him. And he could see her. See right to her core.

Alessia was so taken by the animalistic beauty of the man making love to her with such ferocious passion that she was hardly conscious of her second climax building inside her until it exploded like a pulsating firework that throbbed and sparkled through her entire being and carried her away to the stars.

It was the ringing of the bell that brought Alessia crashing back down to earth.

Eyes flying open, they locked onto Gabriel's. The

dazed expression she found in them perfectly matched what she was feeling inside.

'That's our dinner,' she whispered.

His brow creased as if he'd never heard of dinner before. The surround of his mouth was smeared red with her lipstick.

She laughed for absolutely no discernible reason. Maybe she was delirious? She didn't care. She felt like she could spring onto a cloud and float into the stratosphere. 'The staff will be bringing our dinner in at any second.'

Firm lips crushed against hers, teeth capturing her bottom lip as he pulled away from her with a growl.

Hastily, they scrambled to make themselves presentable. Alessia had a much easier time of it seeing as she still had her skirt and top on, and she tried to help Gabriel button his shirt but it buttoned differently to what she was used to and she was more a hindrance than a help.

She opened the dining room door and took her seat exactly ten seconds before the servers arrived.

Three days later, the paparazzi were waiting in their usual spot outside the castle grounds. That they pursued them all the way to the airfield where Gabriel's jet awaited them reinforced the impact the release of the wedding statement had had. The royal family always travelled in official cars and were always followed, but the times Gabriel had come and gone from the castle before had evoked only cursory interest from the vultures. Now, even though they were in the back of a non-official car, the paparazzi were clearly taking no chances that their cash cow might be inside it.

When they arrived at his home a few miles north of Madrid a few hours later, his heart sank to find another pack of paparazzi staked outside his estate. Fortunately, they preferred to move out of the way than get run over by his driver.

'I'm sorry,' Alessia whispered, squeezing his hand.

He gave a rueful smile. 'You have nothing to be sorry for. They will get bored soon.'

'I'll only be encroaching your space for a few days. Once I'm back home, they'll leave you alone here.'

His next smile was grim. Bringing her hand to his mouth, he kissed it and inhaled heavily. Alessia's birth and the resultant attention it brought her was not her fault. She played the media game because it went hand in glove with her role but she didn't court publicity for personal vanity like his mother did. He should never have made her feel bad for something that was beyond her control.

'You are my wife and what's mine is yours, which means this is your home too,' he told her seriously. 'Don't ever think you're not wanted here or not wanted by me.'

Her eyes held his. Her chest rising as slowly as the smile on her face, she placed a palm to his cheek and a dreamy kiss to his mouth. 'Thank you,' she said when she pulled her mouth away. 'I needed to hear that.'

He kissed her. 'And I needed to say it.'

It astounded him how quickly things could change. Opinions. Feelings. Desires.

Before their wedding a week ago, the thought of Alessia in his home had made his chest tight. Now, it was knowing that on Sunday she would fly back to Ceres without him that made it tighten.

Before their wedding, he'd known he wanted to be a good husband and a good father but they had been driven by the circumstances of their child's conception. His own father had been a good father—those two years of warfare with his mother not withstanding—and Gabriel wanted to give the same feeling of love and security to his own child. As he knew how damaging it could be for a child to witness parents at war, he knew the best way to achieve love and security for his child was by being a good husband.

The more time he'd spent with Alessia and the more he'd got to know the woman behind the princess mask, though, the more he wanted to be a good husband for her sake too. He wanted to make her happy for her own sake. Nothing made his heart lighter than to see her smile and hear her laugh.

Was he falling in love with her? It was a question he'd asked himself more and more since they'd become lovers.

Three days, that's all it had been. Three days of hedonistic bliss that had blown his mind, but it had been a hedonism that had to be rationed to the evenings and nights. Here, in his Madrid home, there was nothing to stop them spending their entire days and nights making love, and he imagined all the places they could…

'Oh, my, your *house*!'

For the first time in three days, Alessia found her attention grabbed by something that wasn't entirely Gabriel. They'd driven past the security gates and now she was trying to stop her mouth gaping open. Surrounded by high, thick trees for privacy, white-edged cubes infilled with glass were cleverly 'stacked' to create a postmodern structure like nothing she'd seen before. Where the castle her family had called home for five hundred years was believed to have had the first wing built around a thousand years ago, this home could be set a thousand years into the future.

Driven into a subterranean car park with a fleet of gleaming supercars lined up, a glass elevator took them up to the next level. A butler was there to greet them. Other than shaking his hand at the introduction, Alessia was still too dazed about the futuristic world she'd just landed in to summon her Spanish and follow the conversation.

'Are you okay?' Gabriel asked, an amused smile on his face, once the butler had left them in a vast white living area that looked as if it would repel dust from fifty paces.

She shook her head, noticing an abstract bronze sculpture taller than Gabriel that she was sure was the one that had made the news earlier in the year by breaking records when it had been sold at auction. 'I'm just trying to take everything in. I've never seen anything like your home before…' Movement caught her eye and she turned her head and did a double take. 'Is that a *waterfall*?'

She hurried over to the wall of windows the water was pouring down outside of, but before she'd reached it, the glass began to slide open. Still shaking her head, she stepped out into a vast outdoor area with plentiful seating and plentiful sun loungers that lined a long swimming pool the waterfall was falling into. Craning her neck, she gave a squeal to find there was another glass swimming pool jutting out over her.

'It's a trio of infinity pools,' Gabriel explained, standing beside her. 'The one above us extends from the private balcony in our bedroom.'

Walking to the edge of the decking area, Alessia looked down over the glass perimeter railing and saw the third swimming pool.

'That one extends from the spa,' Gabriel told her. 'There's an indoor one too, for when the weather is cooler.'

'Amazing,' she breathed, still craning her neck up and down to take the three infinity pools in. The top one was the shortest and narrowest, the bottom the longest and widest, which she guessed meant the swimmer could swim in the sun or the shade on the lower two levels. 'I've spent twenty-three years begging my parents to have an outdoor swimming pool put in but they always say no because they fear it will ruin the picture-perfect architecture of the castle. And you've got three!'

'I like to swim.'

Now she gave him all of her attention and happily let her gaze soak him in. 'I can tell.' It felt amazing to be able to do that, to let her eyes run over him whenever she wanted and say whatever was on her mind which, admittedly, had mostly been sex these last few days. It felt even more amazing that the heady feelings that had become such an intrinsic part of her were reciprocated. Alessia had fallen headfirst into lust with her own husband and it was the best feeling in the world. 'I wish you'd told me. I'd have brought a swimming costume with me.'

A lascivious gleam appeared in his eyes. 'Who needs a swimming costume when we have all this privacy?'

The mere thought made her legs go weak. 'What about your staff?' she asked, suddenly breathless.

'All chores are done in the morning. Gregor—the butler—has a self-contained apartment at the back of the kitchen that he shares with the chefs. They don't come into the main house unless I call for them.' He dipped his head and ran his tongue over the rim of her ear. 'We have complete privacy.'

Stepping onto her tiptoes, she hooked her arms around his neck and rubbed her nose into his neck, filling her senses with the scent of his skin she was rapidly becoming addicted to. 'Complete privacy?'

He clasped her bottom and pulled her to him. 'I could take you now and no one would know.'

The outline of his excitement pressed against her abdomen almost flooded her with an urgent, sticky heat.

'Then do it,' she whispered, grazing her teeth into his skin. 'Take me now.'

Minutes later, lifted and pressed against the wall, her legs wrapped tightly around Gabriel's waist as he pounded into her and the pulses of a climax thickened inside her, Alessia dreamily wondered who this wanton woman who'd taken possession of her body was.

CHAPTER ELEVEN

LATER THAT AFTERNOON, when Gabriel had to drag himself away from making love to return some of the calls he'd neglected these last few days, Alessia took herself off exploring. There was so much to see! To her delight, by the time she'd finished exploring the villa's interior, Gabriel was sitting on the balcony having a drink.

'Your home is amazing,' she said, sinking into the seat next to his and twisting round to face him, unable to keep the smile from her face. As well as the huge living area, there was a smaller, cosier living room, a cinema room with sofas so deep and wide a party of people could sleep on them, a games room with a bar, other bars inside and out, a full-blown gym and a spa area bigger than the ground floor of her quarters. On top of all that were the eight bedrooms, eleven bathrooms, an upper floor entertainment area... It was endless! Oh, and Gabriel's office, which she'd only peeked into to blow a kiss at him as he was on a call. Oh, and there were two kitchens too, an indoor one which looked like it belonged on a spaceship, and an outdoor one. She hadn't even thought of exploring the grounds yet!

His eyes crinkled. 'I'm glad you like it,' he said as he poured her a glass of iced water and passed it to her.

She thought of the intricate sketches he'd made of the stables. 'Did you design it yourself?'

'I had the vision of what I wanted but an architect put those visions into something workable.'

'It's the polar opposite of the castle. And I can't get over how quiet it is.' She closed her eyes and listened hard. The castle was quiet at night but by day, it being a place of work as well as her family's home, it bustled with the burr of people's voices, footsteps and general movement.

Large hands wrapped around her ankles and pulled her feet onto his lap. 'How would you feel about us turning the stables into something like this?'

She met his stare with a mournful sigh that turned into a sigh of pleasure when he began rubbing his thumbs over her left calf. 'We'd never be allowed— can you imagine this there? Much as I love this, it wouldn't fit in with the surroundings.'

'Agreed, but with some clever architecture, we can get a lot more light into it.'

Relaxing under his strong, manipulating fingers, she sighed again. 'That would be nice. I've never really considered how little natural light there is in the castle. I don't suppose anyone thought about natural light when they converted the stables either. They probably thought my grandmother's personality suited living in darkness,' she added with a cackle of laughter.

'I'm still astounded by what you told me of her.'

'That she hated being a royal?'

'No, I understand that; but that she seemed to hate people including her own family.'

'She didn't *seem* to, she *did* hate people.'

'Including your mother?'

'I suppose she must have loved her,' she said doubtfully. 'That's what mother's do, isn't it? Love their children.'

His fingers were still working their magic on her legs, now massaging the muscles of her right calf. 'You don't sound sure.'

'I'm not. It's not something we really talk about. I know my grandmother was hard on my mother but she was hard on everyone. She wasn't a woman for drying a child's tears, but she knew her duty and she was the perfect queen consort. She never let my grandfather down.'

'Not until he died.'

'But when he died my mother took the throne and my father became consort. My grandmother was relegated to dowager queen. She gave forty years of her life to our monarchy so I don't blame her for wanting to retire from the public eye and wanting some privacy away from the castle.'

'You sound like you admire her.'

'I do in a way. And I feel sorry for her too. She must have really hated being a royal to go to those extremes once her duty was over.'

'And how do you feel about being a royal?'

She shrugged. 'It's just my life, isn't it? I never had a choice about it and I don't know anything different.'

'Have you ever wished for anything different?'

'Not for a long time.'

'But you used to?'

She nodded. 'When I was small.' She gave a quick smile. '*Smaller*. I used to wish my mother wasn't queen.'

'Really?'

'Really. I was six when my grandfather died and everything changed overnight. My mother took the throne but it felt to me that the throne took her. Before, when she was just heir to the throne, she had many responsibilities but she was still able to be a mother to us…in her own way. She never bathed me or read me bedtime stories—my father read me stories, though; he was always much more present, even after she took the throne—but she did take an interest in me. I remember she wanted to see my schoolwork every day—this was when I had a governess, before I went to boarding school—and see for herself that my handwriting was developing properly and that I was learning my sums. Sometimes she made me read to her. Once she took the throne, that all stopped as she just didn't have the time. There were always more important things that needed her attention.'

'That must have been tough for you.'

'It was but it's how royal life works. In our royal family, in any case. Like your mother, she did the best she could. You have to remember who *her* mother was and the upbringing she'd had. She tried hard to create a more loving environment for us in comparison to what she'd endured but there were times when it was very hard. The toughest time was when she went to Australia and New Zealand for two months with my father on a state tour. I was only seven, and it was the first time I'd been properly separated from them. I can't tell you how sick I felt from missing them. It was awful.'

'What would you do if you were asked to do the same thing?'

'Leave our child on a state tour?'

He nodded.

'I wouldn't do it.'

'Why not? They'd be at home with me so they wouldn't be separated from both their parents like you were.'

'But they'd still be without their mother. Do you remember what you said that day about putting our child's wellbeing before duty?'

His eyes narrowed slightly in remembrance.

'Gabriel... I have always put my duty to my family and the monarchy first, above everything. Everything I've ever done has always been with duty and what's expected of me at the forefront of my mind.'

'And wanting approval from your mother?' he asked astutely.

'Maybe... Probably...' She grimaced. 'When I was a child I lived for my mother's attention because I got so little of it.'

'Was being a good princess a way to get it?'

'Yes. She always noticed…complimented me on my deportment and manners.' She expelled a long breath. 'I'd never allowed myself to step out of line before, and it hurts my heart that she's still angry with me about my Dominic comments and the circumstances of the pregnancy. That night… It's the only time I have ever, *ever* put my own desires first. The consequences were so great I thought I would never be able to do anything like that again but I feel the changes happening inside me and think of the child growing in my womb and the *feelings* I have for it…' She shook her head, unable to put into words how strong the emotions were. 'Our child's emotional wellbeing is more important to me than anything. My feelings are the same as yours in that regard—when you've experienced pain, the last thing you want is to put your own child through the same, and I will not make them go through what I went through. If I was asked to go on tour, I would only accept if our child could come with me.'

His hands had stopped working their magic, his stare fixed on her. There was a long pause before his shoulders relaxed and he lightly said, 'But then I would be left at home alone.'

She swallowed. On Sunday night Alessia would fly back to the castle without him, returning to her dutiful place for a full week of royal engagements. Five whole days without him.

Until the stables renovations were complete, this would be her life, only seeing him at weekends. And those precious weekends would be interrupted too, she thought with an ache, when she attended one of her frequent weekend engagements.

Would things be better when they moved into the stables and Gabriel was in a position to work from home? She would still be a princess going about her duty without her prince by her side.

For the first time, the prince of her dreams had a face. Gabriel's.

'You wouldn't have to be alone,' she whispered. 'Any time you change your mind and decide to be my prince—'

'It isn't going to happen,' he said, cutting her off. But there was no malice in his voice, just a simple matter-of-factness with a tinge of ruefulness in it.

'I know.'

'I will not be your prince but I will be your husband.'

She nodded, almost too choked to speak, but she forced herself to say what was on her mind and in her heart. 'I'd love for you to be my prince, I really would.'

Carefully placing her feet back on the floor, Gabriel gripped the sides of her chair and pulled her to him. Once their knees were touching, he ran his fingers through her hair, then gently rubbed his thumb under her chin. 'I know our marriage is not what you grew up expecting your marriage to be. It isn't what I wanted or expected of a marriage either, but we can make it work and we can be happy.'

'I want to believe that.'

Palming her cheeks, a fervour came into his voice.

'Think about it, Lessie. When we move into the stables, we can make it a real home, a real distinction between the princess and the woman. We can make it a home without any intrusion from royal life and all its demands, and our child can have the semblance of a normal life. And so can we.'

The following weekend, Alessia walked out of the bathroom after her shower with the robe wrapped around her, and stepped into the dressing room, where Gabriel had made space for her clothes. He was taking her out, something that thrilled her, just as it thrilled her to be back in his arms after five nights apart. She'd arrived in Madrid late last night and they'd gone straight to bed, making love until the sun had come up. Only when they'd finally woken at midday did he lazily announce that he would be taking her out that night. She'd assumed his aversion to publicity meant she would spend her entire marriage without a single date with her husband.

She wished she dared hope that he would one day change his mind and be her prince as well as her husband, even if it was only for those important family occasions like Amadeo's wedding. She wished so hard he would come with her, a wish that no longer had anything to do with not wanting to be humiliated. Alessia just wanted the man she was falling in love with to be a real part of her family, not the royal side of it but the human side, and to hold her hand and create the same memories of those special occasions together.

But it wasn't going to happen and there was no point upsetting herself over it. Their time together was short and she didn't want to waste it by moping.

Choosing a white, strapless jumpsuit, she happily dressed and set to work on her hair and face. It felt strange to be doing her own beauty care for a night out. Normally the castle beauty team would set to work and turn her into the princess the world expected to see. Gabriel had offered to bring in Madrid's top beautician and hair stylist for her but she'd wanted to try it herself. Here, in Madrid, she could just be Alessia, and it was a novelty that showed no sign of abating.

The thought of returning to the castle without him again sent an even stronger pang through her than it had last weekend.

The five days without him had passed quickly and yet somehow with excruciating slowness. She'd had a couple of engagements each day and one on Wednesday evening, so in that respect, the time had flown, and yet, every time she'd sneaked a peek at her watch, she'd found the time until seeing Gabriel again still very far away.

Never mind, she told herself brightly. She was here now. Make the most of the time with him while she had him, and as she thought that, he strolled into the bedroom.

She beamed, unable and unwilling to contain her delight even though it had been less than an hour since he'd crawled out of bed after making love to her again. 'How's your sister?' she asked.

Gabriel, who'd just spent an hour on the phone to Mariella, tugged his T-shirt up. 'She's doing great. She'll be back next week.' He whipped the T-shirt over his head. Mariella was currently doing a sight-seeing tour of Japan with her on-off lover. 'It's her birthday next Saturday so I've invited her to join us for dinner to celebrate.'

About to drop his shorts, he noticed Alessia's falling face in her reflection at the dressing table.

'What's wrong?' He'd thought Alessia liked his sister. Not that she knew her properly yet, but he wanted her to. Nothing would make him happier than for his wife and his sister to get along and enjoy each other's company.

'I don't think I'll be here next weekend,' she said, reaching for her phone. Swiping, she began to type, saying, 'I'm sure I've got an engagement next Saturday night at the royal theatre. It's an annual variety night raising money for cancer research. I'm just checking now, but I'm sure it's next weekend.'

'If you've got an engagement then you've got an engagement,' he said evenly, even though his heart had sunk at the news. It meant he would have to spend the weekend at the castle, and without Alessia for a large chunk of it. 'It can't be helped.' Striding over to her, he dropped a kiss into her neck. 'I'm going to take a shower and have a shave.'

'Where are we going?'

'Club Giroud.'

'The private members' club?'

'You've been?'

'Not to the one in Madrid, but some friends and I went to the one in Rome last year... You do know it's owned by King Dominic's brother-in-law?'

'I've known Nathaniel Giroud for years.'

She blinked her shock. 'You've never mentioned it.'

He shrugged. 'We're acquaintances. His clubs are a good place to do business.'

Her phone buzzed. She swiped again then lifted her stare back to him and shrugged apologetically. 'Sorry. The theatre engagement is next Saturday.'

'It can't be helped. I'll rearrange Mariella for another weekend.'

'But it's her birthday,' she said, clearly upset about it. Then her face brightened. 'I know! She can come and stay with us at the castle. If she wants, I can arrange a ticket to the show for her.'

'I will ask her.'

She hesitated before quietly saying, 'And you can come too, if you'd like? You wouldn't have to sit with me. I can get you tickets to sit with your sister.'

'You already know the answer to that,' he said evenly. Then, placing another kiss to her neck, Gabriel went into the bathroom and stood under the shower, turning the heat up as high as he could endure.

Away from Alessia's alert eyes he took some deep breaths and willed the bilious resentment out of him.

This was the life he'd signed up for. Alessia's job was a princess. He shouldn't resent that it took her away from him on the few nights they had together.

* * *

The seductive glamour of Madrid's Club Giroud was everything Alessia had expected and more. Situated in an ordinary street with an ordinary façade, having shaken their tail of paparazzi off they entered through an unobtrusive, ultra-discreet yet heavily guarded underground car park.

An elevator took them up to the club proper and then the night began.

First they had a meal in the swish restaurant, dining on the kind of food served up at the castle when honoured guests of state were in attendance, then they explored the rooms, each with its own vibe. In some, business-suited men and women were clearly discussing business but everyone else was there to dance or gamble or sip cocktails with other members of the ultra-rich and powerful, confident that whatever took place within the club's walls stayed there. Having been in existence for almost two decades, the press still hadn't got wind of it and it remained one of the few places a man like Gabriel could let his hair down and relax.

There were many faces Alessia recognised and, as she sipped a glass of fizzy grape juice in the poker room—no alcohol for her during the pregnancy—an elegant figure caught her eye and she elbowed Gabriel. 'Look,' she hissed. 'It's Princess Catalina and her husband.'

Gabriel, about to lay a card down, followed her stare.

As if they could feel their eyes on them, Nathaniel and Catalina Giroud turned their heads in unison. In an instant, smiles of recognition lit their faces and they weaved through the crowds to them.

Rising to his feet, Gabriel shook Nathaniel's hand and, after being introduced, exchanged kisses with Catalina, who then turned her attention to Alessia and smiled widely. 'Little Alessia Berruti! Look at you all grown up...' A flare of mischief crossed her face. 'Although not much taller than I remember.'

'You two have met?' Gabriel asked.

Alessia shrugged sheepishly. 'The royal world is a small world. But it's been a long time,' she added to Catalina. 'I think I was ten when we last met.'

Almost a decade older than Alessia, Catalina took her hand. 'Yes, I remember. It was at your parents' anniversary party. I remember being sorry for you when you were sent to bed. You tried so hard to keep a brave smile on your face and not show your disappointment.'

'I guess I didn't try hard enough if you noticed it,' she laughed.

'I only noticed because I'd once been in your shoes. You carried it off far more successfully than I ever did.'

Agreeing to join them for a drink, Gabriel finished his game and then they set off to the piano room, where a session musician was playing in the corner.

After a fresh round of drinks were served, the conversation soon turned to the one subject he would prefer not to speak of. Amadeo's wedding. Catalina was cousin to the bride. Though it was doubtful she would know of Gabriel's involvement in the setting up of the marriage, his chest still tightened.

'I'm looking forward to it,' Catalina surprised them by saying.

'You're going?' Alessia asked.

'I wouldn't miss it for the world.'

'But Dominic will be there.'

It was no secret in their circle that Dominic used to hit and tyrannise his sister and that he was the principal reason she'd fled Monte Cleure with Nathaniel.

'Forgive me, but I was under the impression you wouldn't step foot in the same country as Dominic.'

Catalina's face clouded. 'I won't ever return to Monte Cleure, not while Dominic's on the throne.' Then she brightened and looked adoringly at her husband, who gave her a meaningful look that only Catalina could understand. 'But I want to see Elspeth married and safely away from him with my own eyes. She was always a sweet little thing, and the wedding's in Ceres and Dominic can't touch me there. If he tried, Nathaniel would kill him.'

Alessia had no doubt Catalina spoke the truth. The love this couple had for each other was as strong as the love she felt emanating from Marcelo and Clara, and she couldn't help herself from glancing at Gabriel, whose hand was wrapped tightly around hers.

Her heart sighed.

Would Gabriel ever feel such a deep-rooted, protective, possessive devotion to her?

She knew he was as crazy for her as she was for him but that was a physical, chemistry-led craziness.

She knew too that the personal dislike he'd once felt for her had gone and that he did like her, very much, and that he intended to be a faithful husband to her.

But love? The kind of love that meant you would do anything for the one you loved, cherish them, and put the other's happiness before your own…?

As she thought this, Catalina said, 'I understand you're a bridesmaid, Alessia.'

Forcing a practiced smile to her face, she nodded. 'Yes. There are five of us altogether.'

'And you, Gabriel?' Catalina asked. 'What role are you playing for the wedding?'

'I'm not,' he replied smoothly. 'I won't be there.'

Even Nathaniel raised a brow at this.

'It was agreed when Alessia and I married that I would remain a private person.'

'But this is your brother-in-law's wedding…' Catalina's voice tailed off, and she took a quick drink of her champagne to cover the awkwardness.

'I'd like you to be there,' Alessia said softly before she could stop herself.

Gabriel's eyes zoomed straight onto hers. For the first time in a long time, the expression on his face was unreadable.

Already regretting her unguarded words, she gave a rueful shrug and squeezed his hand. 'It's okay. I understand why you can't be.'

And she did understand.

But she understood too that Gabriel already knew perfectly well how much she longed for him to be the prince on her arm, especially for that one day.

That he wouldn't even entertain the idea of accompanying her for that one special day told her more than any words that he didn't love her and that, for all his talk about finding happiness and harmony together, her needs could never trump his own.

The burgeoning love growing in her heart was unlikely to ever be reciprocated.

Gabriel prowled the empty quarters of the castle he doubted would ever feel like a home to him. The silence was more acute than usual for this early in the evening. Normally there would be background noise until around ten p.m.

With his sister having turned down Alessia's theatre offer to take a trip to Ibiza, and unable to get into his book, he remembered Alessia saying the variety show was being televised and figured that as he couldn't be with her in person, he could try and catch a glimpse of her in the crowd.

He got his wish almost immediately. An act had just finished, the three members bowing to the audience. The camera panned to the reaction in the royal box, and he understood why the castle was so quiet. The whole family, even Clara, were in attendance.

As he attempted to digest this, his phone vibrated. When he read the message, his mood went from bad to worse.

'What's wrong?' Alessia asked as she slipped her shoes off. After an evening she'd started with such high hopes that her mother would finally show signs of forgiveness, her hopes had been dashed when all Alessia's attempts at conversation were met with terse replies and a turned cheek. Her lifted spirits at returning home to Gabriel had sunk back down before she made it over the threshold of the dayroom where he was holed up. She could practically smell the foulness of his mood. She could certainly smell the scent of bourbon in the air.

The ardent lover who could strip her naked with a look took a long time to respond. When he finally turned his face to her, the only thing his stare would strip was acid.

Wordlessly, he held his phone out to her.

She looked at the page he'd saved on his screen and silently cursed.

Gabriel's mother had sold her story to the press. The whole world now knew the reluctant prince was the son of Monica Binoche. There was no doubt the media circus that had left him alone during the weeks when Alessia was in Ceres without him would now renew its focus. The privacy he cherished could be kissed goodbye for the foreseeable future. And all because his mother had sold him out again. She'd put her need for validation and the spotlight above her son's emotional wellbeing.

He sighed heavily. 'I should have guessed the temptation would be too much for her.'

Feeling wretched for him, she climbed onto the sofa and wrapped her arms around him.

There was a stiffness in his frame she'd not felt

since the night she'd wept on his chest, right before the passion had taken them in its grip.

'I'm sorry,' she whispered, stroking his back. 'I know how hard this must be for you.'

Do you? Gabriel wanted to bite. *Then why did you give me those puppy eyes and tell me you wanted me at Amadeo's wedding? Was it to guilt me?*

But he wouldn't bite. He would never bite. His parents had always bitten at each other, the early passion of their marriage turning into passionate hatred that rained misery on everyone.

Instead, he filled his lungs with all the air he could fit in them and rested his chin on the top of her head, and waited for Alessia's soft fruity scent to work its magic on him.

It didn't.

The fury inside him refused to diminish, his mother's betrayal a scalding wound, and then there was Alessia too, failing to tell him her whole damn family were going to the theatre engagement. She wanted him to break the conditions of their marriage and attend Amadeo's wedding but refused to renege on an engagement for his sister's birthday. As a result, Gabriel had blown his sister out on her birthday so he could snatch a few hours with his wife when it turned out the engagement she 'couldn't' miss was one she actually could have missed because the rest of the damned Berruti royal family, including the queen and her heir, had been there. Alessia's absence would have been minimised.

Duty would always come first to her, he thought bitterly, and disentangled himself from her arms so he could pour himself another bourbon.

CHAPTER TWELVE

GABRIEL'S MOOD HADN'T improved the next day, and when the invitation came to dine with the queen and king in their quarters that evening for a family meal, he bit back yet another cutting remark and reminded himself that these weren't just monarchs, they were his in-laws and the grandparents of the child growing in his wife's belly.

There was a snake alive in *his* belly, a cobra fighting to rise up his throat and strike.

He would not let it out.

He was conscious from the way Alessia was walking on eggshells around him that she was aware of the darkness. Conscious too that his tone was curter than he would like, he tried hard to moderate it and respond to the affection she continued to show him.

Tomorrow morning he was flying back to Madrid. His departure couldn't come soon enough. Some time alone, away from this damn castle, would give him his perspective back. He tried to find some perspective now too.

So his mother had sold him out? Hadn't he been

expecting it? Even his sister, when she'd called to commiserate, had been indulgent in her reaction to their mother's actions. But then, Mariella had never hated the media circus that had followed their childhood and adolescence. She'd hated the fights as much as him and, like him, refused to be drawn into arguments that led to raised voices, but the media didn't bother her in the slightest.

And so Alessia had attended an engagement with her family she could easily have cancelled to spend an evening with his sister for her birthday? In Madrid, Alessia was free to be Alessia. Here, in the ancient castle, she rarely removed her princess skin. It would be easier for the woman to emerge fully when they were living together full-time, and she wouldn't need or want him to be anything more than her husband.

Despite his pep talk to himself, it was with a great deal of trepidation that Gabriel set off with Alessia to her parents' quarters.

He'd dined with the queen and king in their quarters once before, the night his plane was grounded. Then, the meal had been formal, the food and wine as exquisite as anything he'd been served in a Michelin-starred restaurant. That night the food, although served with the usual ceremony, was a lot more homely, slow roasted lamb and ratatouille. The whole atmosphere was much more welcoming and light-hearted, the conversation, too, relaxed.

The only person not relaxing into the atmosphere was Alessia. Seated across from him, she held herself with a straight-backed deportment that would be fitting if it were a state occasion and not a family meal. She wasn't speaking much either, he noted, and every time he caught her eye, her smile seemed forced. The queen, he noted too, wasn't engaging her daughter in conversation, and he thought back to Alessia's comment about her mother still being angry with her over the circumstances of the pregnancy. It was a comment he'd mulled on a number of times as there was something about that whole conversation nagging at him, a feeling that there was something about it he was missing. Something important.

'How are the wedding preparations going?' Clara asked Amadeo.

The heir to the throne pulled a disgruntled face. 'Very well.'

'The whole of Ceres has gone wedding mad,' she said with glee. 'I can't wait! It's a shame I'm not a bridesmaid but I get why I can't be—best not to antagonise King Pig!'

To Gabriel's amusement, even the queen looked like she was trying not to laugh.

'What a shame that despot had to be invited but then it would kind of defeat the purpose of the wedding not to have him there,' Clara continued before whipping her attention to Gabriel. 'Is it true you're not coming?'

'I'm afraid it is true.'

'No *way*? Why's that?'

'Because I wish to remain a private person,' he said tightly, his muscles bunching together. He took a sip of his wine. Why must he continually explain himself?

'I know that, but this is a wedding. How can anyone not love a good wedding? And this will be the wedding of the century. And Elsbeth seems really sweet,' Clara added, looking again at Amadeo, who pulled another disgruntled face. She stuck her tongue out at him, which, to Gabriel's amazement, made everyone, including the perpetually stiff-necked Amadeo, laugh.

Laughing along with them, Gabriel drank some more wine to drown the poised cobra.

'You were quiet tonight,' Gabriel said when they were back in their quarters and finally alone. 'Want to tell me what's on your mind?'

Alessia sank onto the nearest sofa and sighed forlornly. 'Just my mother's attitude towards me. I keep hoping she'll forgive me but there's still no sign of it.'

She kneaded her aching forehead. Alessia's insides had felt knotted from the moment she'd woken. For the first time since they'd become lovers, Gabriel had shared a bed with her and not made love to her. She sensed the demons working their darkness in him and longed for him to open up to her, but she knew what the cause was: his mother's treachery in selling him out. He'd been open with her about that.

But Gabriel was not a man to spill his guts. He'd told her everything about his childhood but had relayed it matter-of-factly. He freely admitted it had made him the man he was but he never spoke about how it had made him feel or how it still made him feel.

She couldn't force it. He would tell her if and when

he was ready. But she'd gone to her parents' quarters feeling knotted in her stomach for her husband, and her mother's welcoming embrace had been delivered in such a detached manner that the knots had tightened so she could hardly breathe, and suddenly she could hold it back no longer.

A jumble of words came rushing out. 'Do you know, my mother has never been angry with Marcelo before, not like she's being with me, and he's the one who started this whole mess. He dangled out of a helicopter to rescue Clara from Dominic's palace, and he was understood and forgiven even before he put things right by marrying her. I made one mistake… okay, two…and I've paid the price for it. I've done everything I can to make amends and even Amadeo's forgiven me, but I can still feel her anger. Marcelo has got away with murder—not literally—over the years, whereas I've always been the good one. I've always been dutiful, always known my place in the family and in the pecking order, never given a hint of trouble, but there's no forgiveness from her for me. She can hardly bring herself to look at me.'

Gabriel listened to her unloading in silence. When she'd got it all out, he sat next to her and took her hand. 'Do you want to know what I think?'

A tear fell down her cheek. She wiped it away and nodded.

'Your mother—all your family—have spent years learning how to temper themselves when Marcelo falls out of line, but you've never stepped out of line before. You've never disappointed them. You've always done your best to live up to your birthright. You've followed in your mother's footsteps and put duty first, above your own wants and feelings.'

'Not as much as Amadeo has.'

'We're not talking about Amadeo, we're talking about you. I don't know if you're fully aware of the impact you have on people—you, more than anyone else in your family, have carried your monarchy into the twenty-first century. You've navigated being a princess with being a modern woman in the age of social media and all without putting a foot wrong and never with a word of complaint, even when you're abused by trolls. Your mother is the queen, Amadeo the heir to the throne, but it is you who captures the public's imagination, and you who the public sees as a princess to her core. I think your family, especially your mother, see you like that too, and so when your human side was revealed so publicly, they did what they always do when the monarchy comes under threat and went straight into damage limitation mode.'

'I don't think my mother likes my human side,' she admitted with a whisper.

'Only because you've never shown it to her before. When we're living in the stables and you have breathing space to remove the princess mask you've always forced yourself to wear, your mother will learn that Alessia the woman is worth a hundred of Alessia the princess. For now, though, your mother doesn't know how to react to you about it on a personal level because…'

A strand of thought jumped at him, cutting Gabriel's words off from his tongue.

He tried to blink the thought away but then the conversation that had been nagging at him interplayed with the stray thought, and his heart began to race.

'Because?' she prompted.

Certain he must be making two plus two into five, he stared at Alessia closely.

Her eyebrows drew together. 'What's wrong?'

'You've never put a foot wrong,' he said slowly. 'Ever. You've never been linked to another man… You told me yourself that the only time you've ever put your own desires first was the night we conceived our child.' His stomach roiling, he hardened his stare. 'Alessia… Was I your first?'

It was the deep crimson that flooded her neck and face that answered Gabriel's question and sent blood pounding to his head.

Letting go of her hand, he rose unsteadily to his feet. 'Why didn't you tell me?'

Her shoulders rose before she gave a deep sigh and shook her head ruefully. 'I'm sorry. I should have told you, I know that, but at the time I was so wrapped up in the moment and all the things you were making me feel…'

Alessia shook her head again from the sheer relief that it was finally out in the open. She hadn't realised how heavily it had weighed on her conscience until now it had lifted.

Whatever had she been afraid of? Gabriel was her husband. He might not love her but he was committed to her. The truth should never be something to be feared. 'I knew if I told you I was a virgin, you would stop.'

One eyebrow rose, his stare searching. 'You're saying you *knew* I would stop?'

'Not consciously at the time. In the moment… I wasn't thinking. I remember I didn't *want* to think.' She closed her eyes as memories of their first night together flooded her. For the first time in a long time, there was no bitterness at the aftermath. At some point, she didn't know when, she'd forgiven him for that. 'You touched me and I exploded. It was the first time in my whole life that I ever threw off the shackles of Princess Alessia and became just Alessia.'

There was a long pause of silence.

'Then it's a real shame you won't throw the princess shackles off for me now, isn't it?'

It was the underlying bite beneath the smooth veneer of his voice that made her gaze fly back to him. 'What do you mean by that?'

Jaw clenched, he stared at her for an age before giving a curt shake of his head. 'It doesn't matter.'

'You wouldn't have said it if it didn't.'

'It's nothing. Excuse me but I have an early start. I'm going to bed.'

And then, to her bewilderment, he walked straight out of the room. Moments later his footsteps treaded up the stairs.

Her heart thumping, her head reeling, Alessia palmed the back of her neck wondering what on earth had just happened and what he'd just meant.

There was only one way to find out.

She entered their room as the bathroom door locked.

Gabriel brushed his teeth furiously.

The darkness he'd been fighting had tightened its grip on him, the cobra winding its way to the base of his throat.

This was unbelievable. All this time.

There had been nothing—*nothing*—to indicate Alessia was a virgin.

But you weren't thinking clearly that night, a voice whispered. *Not with your head…*

Teeth done, he took stock of his reflection, breathed deeply and gave himself another pep talk.

The past was the past. Alessia was his wife and his future…

Acrid bile flooded his mouth. He swallowed it away but the bitterness remained.

Closing his eyes, he took one more deep breath and stepped back into the bedroom.

He took one look at his wife perched on the side of the bed facing the bathroom door and all the efforts he'd made to get a grip on his emotions were overturned.

Her stare was steady. 'I need you to tell me what you meant.'

He clenched his jaw. 'Now is not the time.'

'Now *is* the time. I must have done something to warrant that remark, and as a wise half-Spanish, half-French man once said, if you don't tell me what's wrong, how can I fix it?'

The look he gave her could freeze boiling water.

'I know things are tough for you right now,' Alessia said, somehow managing to keep the steadiness in her voice through the thrashing of her heart. 'I know your mother's actions feel like a betrayal, but if I've done something to add to it then you need to tell me so I can put things right. Is it because I didn't tell you I was a virgin? Or is there something else at play?'

His chest rose and fell sharply. A contortion of emotions splayed over his face.

Gabriel gritted his teeth so hard it felt like his molars could snap into pieces. The scalding fury…he could feel it infecting every part of him.

'Did I hurt you that night?' he asked roughly.

Eyes widening, she shook her head violently. 'No. It was wonderful. You know it was.'

'Sorry,' he bit out, 'but this little revelation has made me rethink the whole night. I suppose it explains why you weren't on the pill. Or is that another false assumption?' Somehow Gabriel was hanging onto his temper but the thread of it he clung to was fraying and the control he'd always taken with his speech was slipping out of his reach.

She closed her eyes briefly. 'No, I wasn't on the pill. But you already know that.'

'But you didn't think to tell me that then? In the moment? Before we got carried away?'

'I thought you'd taken care of it.'

'How? By wearing an invisible condom?'

There was a flash of indignancy. 'I didn't know and I didn't think to ask. I was stupid and naïve, I know that, but I wasn't thinking that night and neither were you, and you have no right to be angry with me about it because it's on you just as much as it's on me.'

The thread snapped.

'If you'd told me you were a virgin then none of this would have happened!' he snarled. 'Don't you understand that? Do you not know what you've done? I would never have touched you if I'd known! You've trapped me into a damned marriage I never wanted!'

The colour drained from her face. For the longest time she just stared at him, her mouth opening and closing but nothing coming out.

And then something in her demeanour shifted.

She got to her feet.

Somehow she stood taller than he'd ever seen her.

Padding slowly to him, her words had the same cadence as her pace but her quiet tone was scathing. 'I haven't trapped you into anything. We created a child *together*.'

'You think I don't know that? You think I don't know the blame lies with me too? You pushed aside the fact of your virginity and I pushed aside the fact you were a princess and not a mere flesh and blood woman, and I didn't have the sense to think about contraception, and now I'm trapped in a marriage to a woman I would never have married under any other circumstance. I've given up everything for this, my career, my privacy, my whole damn life!'

'You gave all that up for our child,' she snapped back. 'Remember? If you're trapped then it's in a web of your own making. You married me because you didn't trust me to put our child's wellbeing first.'

He crossed his arms tightly around his chest and leaned down into her face. 'You married me for your damn monarchy.'

'No, I married you for my family because the monarchy means everything to *them*, and so that my child could have its father in its life.'

'You married me so you could continue being the perfect princess and redeem yourself in your mother's eyes because being a princess is all you'll allow yourself to be.'

'Being a princess is who I *am*!'

'No, Alessia, you're my wife too, but you wouldn't even take one night off from your duties for my sister's birthday when no one would have missed you at that show.'

'I'd already committed to it, and how you have the nerve to say that when I gladly offered to have Mariella stay with us…' Pacing the room, she threw her hands in the air. 'You talk about everything you've had to give up, but what about all the things I've had to give up, like a whole future spent being a princess without ever having a prince on my arm? You won't even come to my brother's wedding!'

'You knew my conditions before you agreed to our marriage,' Gabriel raged. His unleashed fury and Alessia's passionate defence of herself had his blood pumping through him in a way that seemed to be feeding his anger.

'Conditions without compromise, that's what they

were, and I wasn't allowed to impose any of my own, was I? As with our wedding and the home we live in, I wasn't given a say. I had no choice because you gave me no choice. You talk a good talk about compromise but you won't compromise on Amadeo's wedding, will you, even when you know how much it would mean to me to have you there.'

'I will not feed those vultures and I will not set a precedent. I don't know how many times I have to say that.'

'A precedent?' she cried. 'You call me a flesh and blood woman and then talk about precedents as if I'm nothing but some business contract?'

'The woman I made love to that night was Alessia Berruti. *She's* the woman I committed myself to, the woman I made clear to you that I was marrying, but she's not the woman I find myself married to, not when we're here. The minute you step foot on Ceres your princess mask slips back on and everything becomes about duty, but I have committed myself and so I'm condemned to spend the rest of my life on this damned island hoping every day for a glimpse of the woman I thought I'd married. But you won't throw those princess shackles off again, will you? Not if it means disappointing your mother again. I will always come second to your damned monarchy and your need to always be Princess Perfect so that you can bask in your mother's approval.'

'It's not just for her! It's who I am!'

'It doesn't have to be! Look how good things are between us when we're away from this place. If you step away from your royal duties we can have that all the time.'

She stopped pacing and stared at him with shock. 'Step away from being a princess?'

'Why not?' The thought of his wife quitting her royal duties was not something Gabriel had ever given serious consideration to, but now that the words were out, he grasped at them, for in that moment they made perfect sense. 'You've played your part for your family. Marcelo's married. Amadeo's marrying soon. That's two new beautiful Berruti princesses for the public to fall in love with, and soon no doubt new royal babies. You and I can build a new life away from here where you can be whoever you want to be.'

Alessia's early pregnancy sickness had ebbed and flowed since the hormones of conception had kicked in. The nausea in her belly was the strongest she'd known it since the day they'd agreed the contract for their marriage. 'Are you serious?'

'Yes. You, me and our baby, away from this castle building our own private life together. You can take that princess mask off for ever and just be the woman I adore. What do you say?'

Eyes not leaving his face, she slowly wrapped her arms across her stomach. 'If I consider it, will you consider coming to Amadeo's wedding?'

He laughed. 'If you come round to my way of thinking, neither of us will have to attend his wedding. I know you still feel guilty for your part in its being.'

She held his stare for a long time, tightening her

hold around her abdomen. 'But I want to go. It's my brother's wedding. And I want you to be there too, as my husband, to hold my hand and support me, because yes, I do still feel some guilt for it. But it's not just about guilt. I want you there for *my* sake, as my prince, for the biggest celebration our island's had since my mother's coronation.' She took a long breath and quietly added, 'Come with me, please. Be my husband and my prince for just that one day.'

She held her breath.

For a long time nothing was said between them. Not verbally. The flickering in his eyes told her more than words could ever say.

Now Alessia was the one to laugh, although there was no humour in it. 'You accuse me of putting you second but I wouldn't have to if you'd meet me half-way and just be my prince for family functions. I can't help that there's always press there too, but you knew it before you imposed that condition. I have no choice but to keep a huge chunk of my life separate from you because I *am* a princess, and this is the situation you've created, not me, and now you want me to give up who I am without meeting me even a fraction of the way.' She shook her head. 'You set me up for a fall right from the beginning. You engineered things in our marriage so I have no choice but to put you second.'

A flare of anger crossed his features. 'That is ridiculous.'

'Your mother always put you second, didn't she, until you gave her that final ultimatum.' Strangely, the more she spoke, the calmer she was feeling and the clearer she was seeing. 'Is that what I can expect from you as the next step? An ultimatum that you'll divorce me or take our child from me if I don't agree to step back from the world I was born into?'

'Absolutely not!' he refuted angrily.

'Maybe not consciously,' she accepted with a shrug. No, she didn't believe this had been done at a conscious level any more than she'd not told him of her virginity at the time. 'What you engineered with your conditions, intentionally or not, has become a self-fulfilling prophecy for you and an excellent excuse to keep me at a distance.'

'Do you have any idea how insane that sounds?' he sneered. But the pulse throbbing on his jaw told a different story.

'Is it? Do you realise this is the first time I've heard you raise your voice or lose your temper? You always have to be in control, don't you? The only time you let your emotions out is in the bedroom. What are you afraid of, Gabriel? That the toxicity of your parents' marriage will somehow be ours? Well, I guess that's become a self-fulfilling prophecy for us too. I don't think you're afraid of the press or that you even hate them. I think your refusal to engage with them is your way of punishing your mother because you ended the war between your parents but never dealt with its casualties—you and Mariella. You never dealt with the neglect you were put through, and you were neglected, Gabriel. You and Mariella both. So you punish your mother by refusing to play the game you hate her for but you can't hate her, can you? Not when you love her. So you punish me instead, only committing part of yourself to me, and condemning me to a life with a husband who refuses to be my husband in public, and then you dress it up to salve your conscience by trying to convince yourself that our marriage will be happy once we separate the woman from the princess…'

Alessia took another breath for the strength to continue. 'But the woman and the princess cannot be separated. The woman and the princess are one and the same thing. We cannot be separated because we are one. Ironically, you're the one who brought that woman out in me and it's through our time together that I've learned I *can* embrace both those sides of me. Maybe one day my mother will learn to embrace them too and start accepting my human side. I don't know. I don't think it even matters any more. If she loves me then she must love all of me. I am a princess. I was born a princess. I will die a princess. A princess. Woman. Human. All I have done my entire life is put everyone else's needs and feelings above my own. But for once, today, I will put myself above duty. I will not live with a man who wants to split me in two. I deserve someone who can love all of me… And that someone isn't you.'

Feeling herself in danger of crumbling, needing to keep a tight hold of her falling strength, Alessia moved her folded arms up so they covered her chest, and held his now ashen stare. 'Do you know who you remind me of? My grandmother. She hated the royal game and that twisted her and turned into hate for everyone associated with it, so let me save you a life of misery and free you from the trappings of a marriage you detest. Get in your jet and fly back to Madrid, and never come back.'

The last bit of colour in his face drained away.

'You don't need to be here any more. You know perfectly well that I will put our baby's emotional needs first even without your influence. I'm sure we can come up with a good "compromise" about custody but that's in the future. Right now, I'm going to Marcelo's quarters so you can pack your things and go.'

Marcelo, his domestic staff dismissed for the evening, opened the door to his quarters. Alessia looked into the eyes of the only member of her blood family who'd even tried to understand her and collapsed onto the floor in tears.

CHAPTER THIRTEEN

His butler's voice telling him that his sister had turned up at his home unannounced made Gabriel close his eyes and breathe deeply. He returned the phone receiver to the cradle and refocused on the documents sent by his lawyer for him to read through.

Mariella let herself into his office without bothering to knock.

'I did tell you I was too busy to see you,' he said, pre-empting her.

'You did,' she agreed cheerfully, draping herself on his office armchair. 'But seeing as it's Friday evening and you're here in Madrid and not in Ceres, and you've been avoiding me all week, I decided to put off my dinner date and ignore your edict. Going to tell me what's going on?'

'There is nothing going on.' He dropped his gaze back to his paperwork and made a point of crossing a line out in heavy black marker pen.

'Then why aren't you in Ceres? The wedding's tomorrow.'

'Yes, and as I told you and everyone else, I will not be attending.'

She was silent for such a long time that Gabriel felt compelled to look back up at her. Hunched forwards, elbows on her thighs, chin in the palms of her hands, her stare was speculative.

'What?' he asked tersely.

Her eyes narrowed. 'I know you're a stubborn thing, but I did think on this one occasion you would change your mind.'

'Then you thought wrong.'

'And what about Alessia?'

'What about her?'

'Don't play dumb, Gabriel. It doesn't suit you.'

He struck another black line through the document. He didn't even know what clause he'd just struck out. 'Alessia and I have agreed to part ways,' he told her, and blacked out another line.

His sister's unnatural silence made him look at her again.

'It's for the best,' he told her. 'Our lives are not compatible. We will agree to custody arrangements for our child nearer the—'

His words were cut off when Mariella jumped up from her seat and snatched the documents off his desk. Seconds later, she'd thrown them out of the window.

'What in hell do you think you're doing?' she raged before he could ask that very same question of her. 'What is *wrong* with you? The woman you love is thousands of miles away preparing for one of the biggest days of her life—the coverage of the wedding is *everywhere.* I know you can't stand the media but how can you let her go through that alone?'

Completely unnerved to witness his sister lose her temper, something he could never remember seeing her do before, he said, 'I just told you, we've separated.'

'Then get yourself back to Ceres and un-separate yourselves before it's too late!'

'It's already too late. She's made her mind up and I agree with her. We are not compatible. Alessia's life is one of duty and that is not—'

'And what about your duty to her as a husband?' Mariella demanded, stamping her foot for emphasis. 'What happened to your conviction that you could make your marriage work?'

'I was wrong.'

She stamped her foot again. Gabriel had the strong feeling she wished it was his head under it. 'Since when have you told lies and since when have you quit at anything? You have succeeded at everything you've ever set out to achieve and more—if you'd wanted to make your marriage work then you would have done.'

'I *did* want it to work.'

'Then why are you sitting here pretending to work while your marriage falls apart, you idiot?' Slamming her hands on his desk, she leaned over so her face was right in his. 'I have never seen you as happy as you were with her. I could even hear it in your voice. I was so *happy* for you. It gave me hope that maybe there might be someone out there prepared to take on the screw-up that is me. You found the happiness that I would *kill* for and now you're throwing it away? You married a princess, Gabriel. You knew what the deal was. Either you accept that fully and embrace it or you can look forward to a life as miserable as the one our mother leads.'

'Our mother's life is not miserable.'

'Of course it is! She has two children who both love her and have always forgiven her, and still she can only find succour from the adulation of strangers. If that's not a miserable life then what is it?'

'A selfish one.'

'That too, yes! And the path you're heading right now is going to be just as selfish and lonely and miserable as hers is.'

Gabriel couldn't stop thinking of Mariella's loss of temper. The quarter bottle of bourbon he'd drunk since she'd stormed out of his villa had done nothing to numb his brain.

As much as he wished to plead ignorance and deny any of what she'd said, he knew it was her perception that he was throwing happiness away that had made her see red. Mariella's life revolved around finding her personal Holy Grail. Happiness.

His sister's imagination was as overactive as his wife's.

His estranged wife.

His guts clenched painfully. He had another swig of bourbon.

He'd felt no need to argue back with his sister. He'd felt a little like a spectator watching a usually passive animal in a zoo suddenly start behaving irrationally. Not like it had been with Alessia.

He closed his eyes as their ferocious argument replayed itself. His blood pumped harder to remember how that had felt.

After decades spent containing and controlling his emotions, he'd finally met his match. He couldn't hide himself from Alessia. God knew he'd tried. God knew it was impossible.

Alessia brought the full spectrum of human emotion out in him…

He straightened sharply, jerking his crystal glass so bourbon spilled over his lap. As the liquid soaked into his trousers, his mind cleared.

His sister's perception that he was throwing away happiness had been no view. It had been a fact.

And Alessia's view that he'd sabotaged their marriage had been a fact too. Her reasoning, though, was only partly right.

He'd sabotaged it because Alessia made him feel too damn much, and she had from the moment she'd stepped out of the shadows and into the moonlight on the balcony. She'd broken down every inch of barrier he'd installed to protect himself with, and slipped under his skin.

He had no reason to put those barriers back up. He didn't need to protect himself any more. Not from Alessia. She would never use him as a prop or put her needs ahead of his. He doubted she'd ever put her needs above anyone else's in her entire life. She didn't *want* him as a prop. She only wanted him for himself.

He'd been too scared to let go and give her what she needed from him: the whole of himself. She'd offered him the whole of herself, and instead of getting down on his knees and worshipping the goddess in her entirety as she deserved, he'd selfishly demanded she throw the biggest part of herself away.

Ice licked his skin as the magnitude of what he'd done crawled through him like an approaching tsunami coming to drown him.

He'd pushed away the best thing that had ever happened to him.

He'd pushed away the woman he loved.

He'd pushed away the princess he loved.

With a guttural roar that came from somewhere unknown deep inside him, Gabriel threw the glass as hard as he could. It smashed against the wall and rained down thousands of crystal fragments. His tear-stained image reflected in every shard.

Amadeo's wedding was the first of the three Berruti siblings not to be held in the royal chapel. As heir to the throne, it had been decided with input from the Ceresian government that his position warranted a wedding in the capital city's cathedral. The whole nation had been given a day's holiday to celebrate, and they were out in force, old and young alike lining the entire route from the castle to the cathedral, many wearing the national costume that resembled a brightly coloured poncho, most waving the national flag, and all cheering.

Alessia and the four supremely excited small cousins who made up the other bridesmaids followed the horse-drawn carriage carrying the bride and the man giving her away: the King of Monte Cleure. Alessia and Clara had privately agreed earlier that morning— and Alessia made sure their conversation was entirely private—that Elsbeth would probably run down the aisle to get away from him. Any nagging fears that Elsbeth was being forced into this marriage were dispelled by the excitement shining in her eyes and all over her pretty face.

On that, Gabriel had been right.

She pushed thoughts of him away and continued waving to the cheering crowd.

Today was a day of celebration. Having spent a little time with the bride, she'd become increasingly convinced that she was a woman her brother could fall in love with…if he allowed himself to. Amadeo had a strong streak of stubbornness in him and was quite capable of denying himself happiness if it meant he didn't have to admit he was wrong.

Whether Amadeo fell in love with her or not, Alessia was determined to welcome Elsbeth into the Berruti family and make her feel that she belonged.

Gabriel could have belonged too if he'd allowed it.

Gabriel could go to hell.

The spineless coward hadn't called her. After the way he'd ghosted her before, she shouldn't be surprised. She'd sent him a message giving him the date, place and time of their baby's first scan next week. He hadn't responded. It was on him if he wanted to be there.

Little Carolina, five years old and adorable with a thick mane of black corkscrew hair, spotted someone in the crowd she knew and would have jumped out of the carriage to greet them if Alessia's reflexes hadn't been so good.

Pulling the excitable child onto her lap, she hugged her close and blinked back a hot stab of tears.

No crying today.

It didn't matter how often she told herself that he wasn't worth her tears, they still flooded her face and soaked her pillow every night.

Oh, please don't let him ghost me again. Let him come to the scan, she prayed. *As painful as it is, I can live without him, but my baby shouldn't have to live without him in its life too. That wouldn't be fair. My baby deserves its father.*

The only light in the dark that had become Alessia's life was that her mother had been markedly warmer to her, her maternal compassion roused by the sudden implosion of Alessia's marriage. For once, there had been no talk about damage limitation. Alessia suspected that was Marcelo's doing.

Her relationship with her mother felt like a fresh start.

Her marriage hadn't lasted long enough for its ending to be stale.

She missed him as desperately as if she'd spent her whole life with him.

The carriages arrived in the piazza the cathedral opened onto.

Placing a kiss on the top of her little cousin's head,

she fixed a great smile onto her face and herded the other bridesmaids off the carriage, the driver helping them down one by one.

The flash of cameras was so great that it blurred into one mass of light.

Organising the bridesmaids, Alessia directed them to wave at the screaming, excited crowd and then it was time to follow the bride and King Pig into the cathedral.

The packed congregation got to its feet.

As the bridal party began its long march, Alessia's smile turned into something real as she noticed the spring in Elsbeth's feet. The bride really was fighting the urge to run to Amadeo and demand the bishop get straight to the 'I do's.

Alessia was halfway down the aisle when a tall figure in the family section at the front made her heart thump and then pump ice in her veins.

The cathedral began to sway beneath her feet. If not for the small hands clasped in hers, she would have stumbled.

It took everything she had to keep putting one shaking foot in front of the other. The closer she got, the clearer his features became.

His eyes were fixed directly on her.

The ice in her veins melted and began to heat rapidly. By the time Elsbeth took Amadeo's hand and the bridesmaids' mothers beckoned them to their seats, her whole body was burning, her heart beating like a hummingbird in her chest.

That was her family in their pride of place, the

women in the perfect royal attire for a wedding, the men in identical long-tailed charcoal morning suits. Her father. Her mother. Her brother Marcelo. Her sister-in-law, Clara. Her husband...

He held a hand out to her. His features were tight but his eyes were an explosion of gold.

Her hand slipped into his without any input from her brain.

The service began.

Alessia didn't hear a word of it.

Her body went into autopilot, standing and sitting as directed, singing the hymns, clapping politely when the groom kissed the bride. It stayed on autopilot as they filed out of the cathedral, tipped confetti and rice over the happy-ish couple, smiled for the numerous photos that were taken. And it remained in autopilot in the carriage she shared with Gabriel, Marcelo and Clara, all waving at the cheering crowds, back to the castle and throughout the entire wedding banquet.

Gabriel could see Alessia was in shock and was working entirely in princess mode. She ate and conversed, laughed when appropriate, but she'd shut something off in herself. Even when he spoke directly to her she answered politely but there was a dazed quality to her eyes and no real engagement. It was as if he were a not particularly interesting stranger she'd been paired with for the day.

The banquet ended. The five hundred guests moved into the adjoining stateroom where the evening party was being held. Decorated in golds and silvers that shimmered and glittered from floor to ceiling, the round tables with no official place-settings quickly filled. He followed Alessia to the one she joined Marcelo and Clara at. They exchanged a significant look and then Marcelo fixed his stare on Gabriel.

The look clearly said, 'Fix things now or I will do what I would have done if my wife hadn't taken pity on you and made me help you today: I will throw you out of a window.'

He wouldn't blame him. It was nothing less than he deserved.

The bride and groom took to the dance floor.

Alessia's knuckles whitened around her glass of water.

Gabriel's heart splintered.

The first dance finished.

Gabriel got to his feet and tapped Alessia's shoulder.

She looked at him expressionlessly.

His heart beating fast, he extended his palm to her. 'May I have this dance?'

She continued to stare at him. With no movement on her face, she looked slowly down to his hand then back to his eyes. But still not seeing. Not seeing him.

By now convinced that she wasn't even going to dignify him with an answer, electricity jolted through him when she pressed her fingers into his palm and rose gracefully to her feet.

He closed his fingers around hers before she could change her mind.

Leading her to the slowly filling dance floor, cameras flashing all around them, he slid his hands around her slender waist.

There was a too-long hesitation before she looped her hands loosely around his neck and turned her cheek so that she wasn't looking at him. Other than her hands, not an inch of her body touched his.

But she was there with him. Dancing with him.

Swaying softly to the music, he spoke in a low voice so only she could hear him. 'I love you, Princess Alessia Berruti. I love all of you, the passionate woman and the dignified princess. I love your sense of duty. I love your loyalty. I love your laugh and your sense of the absurd. I love that you can make me laugh. I love that I can make you laugh. I love your voice. I love your eyes. I love your lips and your smile. I love how it feels when I touch you and how it feels when you touch me. I love that you're carrying my child...'

Still swaying, her face slowly lifted. Her eyes locked onto his. The dazed sheen had gone but there was still no expression.

Another splinter broke off his heart and he sucked in a breath before continuing. 'But there are things I hate too. I hate that I left you sleeping that morning. I hate that I never called you back. I hate the conditions I put on our marriage. I hate that I didn't consider your feelings when I imposed them. I hate that our wedding was tiny and sparse. I hate that I was arrogant enough to think that you could ever be anything but the woman you are, and I *hate* that I let you believe you would suit me better as anything other than the woman you are.'

A tear rolled down her cheek.

'I hate that my selfish insecurities tried to hoard you all to myself. I hate that I'm a blind, pig-headed fool who pushed away the best thing that ever happened to him.'

Still holding her waist with one hand, Gabriel reached into his back pocket and pulled out a scrap of paper. Taking one of her hands in his, he placed the paper in it.

She dipped her gaze to it before closing it tightly in her fingers then locked back on him, another tear falling.

'My PA gave me this within minutes of you calling me,' he told her, staring deep into her shining eyes. 'I've kept it in my wallet ever since. I tried to destroy it once. Scrunched it up and threw it in the bin. I went back to the hotel room for it. Alessia…' A sharp lump had formed in his throat and he had to close his eyes and swallow it away before he could continue. 'Lessie, I don't know if love at first sight exists but the first time I looked at you it felt like I'd been struck by lightning. You were everything I thought I didn't want but the truth is you're everything I need. All of you. The princess and the woman. The whole of you. I can't live without you.'

His voice caught and he had to take another moment to compose himself enough to speak. 'I can't live without you,' he repeated, choking and now completely unable to control it. 'Please, Alessia, forgive me. Take me back. Please, I beg you. I am nothing without you. I can't go on like this. You are everything to me. I beg you, give me a chance to put things right. Give me a chance to prove that I can be the husband you deserve and the prince you need…'

'Shh.' A delicate finger was placed on his lips.

It took a beat for him to register that Alessia had closed the gap between them, another beat to register that her tear-filled face was shining at him.

'Oh, Gabriel.' Alessia gazed at the man she'd fallen in love with long before she'd even known it, feeling like she could choke on the emotions that had cracked through her frozen heart and were erupting inside her.

The eyes boring into hers… What she saw in them…

Oh, but it filled her with the glowing warmth of his love.

Dropping the slip of paper, she rose onto her toes, wound her arms around his neck and pressed her nose into the base of his strong throat.

He loved her.

With her lungs filled with that wonderful Gabriel scent she loved so much, she tilted her head back so she could look again into the eyes that always glistened with such wonderful colour.

She would look into them every day for the rest of her life.

'I love you,' she whispered. 'With all my heart.'

He closed his eyes as if in prayer.

Loosening one of her hands from his neck, she slid

her fingers down his arm and clasped them around his hand.

She smiled up at him. 'Kiss me,' she whispered dreamily. 'Kiss me, dance with me and love me for ever.'

Then she closed her eyes as the heat of his breath filled her senses.

His lips brushing tenderly against hers, Gabriel held her in his arms on the dance floor until the music stopped. And then he loved her for ever.

EPILOGUE

BEAMING SO HARD she thought her face might split in two, Alessia gripped tightly to Gabriel's hand as they walked back up the aisle, their vows renewed. The young bridesmaids who'd carried the twelve-foot train of her wedding dress grinned with varying degrees of gappiness. A heavily pregnant Clara, who'd been tasked with keeping the young bridesmaids in order as part of her chief bridesmaid role, looked like she was only just controlling her urge to jump over the nearest congregants and enthusiastically throw herself into Alessia's arms.

Outside in the royal chapel gardens, the sun shone down on the happy couple and their two hundred guests. To Alessia's glee, the sun's rays were diffused by the avalanche of confetti that was tipped over them, started by Gabriel's best man, his sister, Mariella. The only guest who didn't join in was Alessia's mother, but that was only because she had Alessia and Gabriel's three-month-old daughter, Mari, in her arms. The queen's happiness radiated so strongly

Alessia felt its waves on her skin every bit as much as the sun's.

After the professional photographer, who'd been paid a small fortune and made to sign a secrecy order so as to keep this special day entirely private, had finished herding them all into varying orders for the pictures, they all headed inside for the wedding banquet and after-party. When she caught Gabriel's mother surreptitiously taking photos of the party on her phone and realised he'd clocked her too, their eyes met. He shrugged in a 'what else can we expect?' way, and then burst out laughing. Her husband still loathed the press but had become far more adept at tolerating them. Once, he'd even given them a smile that didn't look completely like a grimace.

When the early hours came and the time for dancing and celebrating was over, an exhausted Alessia walked the lit path back to the stables, holding tightly to her husband's hand. Every single person she loved had been there to celebrate the love she and Gabriel had found together.

When they reached their huge oak front door, she was about to take the first step up to it when the ground moved beneath her feet and she found herself swept up into Gabriel's arms.

'I do believe it's traditional for the groom to carry the bride over the threshold,' he murmured, nuzzling his nose into her cheek.

She smiled dreamily at him. 'Thank you, Prince Gabriel.'

'No, Princess Alessia. Thank you.'

She tightened her hold around his neck and pressed her cheek against his. 'Take me to bed.'

'With pleasure.'

* * * * *

#4049 HER CHRISTMAS BABY CONFESSION
Secrets of the Monterosso Throne
by Sharon Kendrick

Accepting a flight home from a royal wedding with Greek playboy Xanthos is totally out of character for Bianca. Yet when they're suddenly snowbound together, Bianca chooses to embrace their deliciously dangerous chemistry, just once...only to find herself carrying a shocking secret!

#4050 A WEEK WITH THE FORBIDDEN GREEK
by Cathy Williams

Grace Brown doesn't have time to fantasize about her boss, Nico Doukas...never mind how attractive he is! But when she accompanies him on a business trip, the earth-shattering desire between them makes keeping things professional impossible...

#4051 THE PRINCE'S PREGNANT SECRETARY
The Van Ambrose Royals
by Emmy Grayson

Clara is shocked to discover she's carrying her royal boss's baby! The last thing she wants is to become Prince Alaric's convenient princess, but marriage will protect their child from scandal. Can their honeymoon remind them that more than duty binds them?

#4052 RECLAIMING HIS RUNAWAY CINDERELLA
by Annie West

After years of searching for the heiress who fled just hours after their convenient marriage, Cesare finally tracks Ida down. Intent on finalizing their divorce, he hadn't counted on the undeniable attraction between them! Dare they indulge in the wedding night they never had?

HPCNMRA0922

#4053 NINE MONTHS AFTER THAT NIGHT
Weddings Worth Billions
by Melanie Milburne

Billionaire hotelier Jack is blindsided when he discovers the woman he spent one mind-blowing night with is in the hospital... having his baby! Marriage is the only way to make sure his daughter has the perfect upbringing. But only *if* Harper accepts his proposal...

#4054 UNWRAPPING HIS NEW YORK INNOCENT
Billion-Dollar Christmas Confessions
by Heidi Rice

Alex Costa doesn't trust *anyone*. Yet he cannot deny the attraction when he meets sweet, innocent Ellie. Keeping her at arm's length could prove impossible when the fling they embark on unwraps the most intimate of secrets...

#4055 SNOWBOUND IN HER BOSS'S BED
by Marcella Bell

When Miriam is summoned to Benjamin Silver's luxurious Aspen chalet, she certainly doesn't expect a blizzard to leave her stranded there for Hanukkah! Until the storm passes, she must battle her scandalous and ever-intensifying attraction to her boss...

#4056 THEIR DUBAI MARRIAGE MAKEOVER
by Louise Fuller

Omar refuses to allow Delphi to walk away from him. His relentless drive has pushed her away and now he must convince her to return to Dubai to save their marriage. But is he ready to reimagine everything he believed their life together would be?

---

*Cesare intends to finalize his divorce to his runaway
bride, Ida. Yet he hadn't counted on discovering Ida's
total innocence in their marriage sham. Or on the
attraction that rises swift and hot between them...
Dare they indulge in the wedding night they never had?*

*Read on for a sneak preview of
Annie West's 50th book for Harlequin Presents,*
Reclaiming His Runaway Cinderella

"Okay. We're alone. Why did you come looking for me?"

"I thought that was obvious."

How could Ida have forgotten the intensity of that
brooding stare? Cesare's eyes bored into hers as if seeking
out misdemeanors or weaknesses.

But she'd done him no wrong. She didn't owe him
anything and refused to be cowed by that flinty gaze. Ida
shoved her hands deep in her raincoat pockets and raised
her eyebrows.

"It's been a long day, Cesare. I'm not in the mood for
guessing games. Just tell me. What do you want?"

He crossed the space between them in a couple of deceptively easy strides. Deceptive because his expression told her it was the prowl of a predator.

"To sort out our divorce, of course."

"We're still married?"

Don't miss
Reclaiming His Runaway Cinderella
available November 2022 wherever
Harlequin Presents books and ebooks are sold.

Harlequin.com